DRIFTWOOD DANGER

SALTWATER COWBOYS, BOOK 5

CHRISTY BARRITT

CHAPTER ONE

ABIGAIL FERGUSON'S eyes flew open only to collide with darkness.

Panic consumed her as confusion preyed on her fears.

Where was she?

This wasn't her bedroom. She was certain of that.

If she were there, her alarm clock would scatter blue light near the edge of her pillow. Her sheets would smell like fruity bergamot. Her white noise machine would croon the lullaby of the ocean.

The rotting scent of decay floated in the air, reminding her of death. A disturbingly still quiet surrounded her. And she felt slumped against something. She wasn't laying down, she realized.

She tried to pull her hands in front of her, to push herself to her feet.

But she couldn't.

Her head fell back against the wall, and she tugged her hands again. They were pinned beside her.

She squinted, trying to get a better look. Ropes looped around her wrists. The ends were attached to something . . . bolted to the wall.

A cry caught in her throat. What was going on?

She squeezed her eyes shut and tried to recall the last thing she could remember.

But she couldn't.

Yet, she *could*.

The memories were right there, on the edge of her consciousness. They taunted her, promising a nightmare she might not recover from. If she invited those thoughts into her head, she might not ever escape from them.

The self-preservation side of herself didn't want the memories to fully emerge. She needed to keep those thoughts far away—for now, at least.

The cry brewing in her lungs emerged as a deep moan.

The darkness held her captive. The frigid cold

assaulted her. She had no idea where she was or how long she'd been here.

Tears tried to press at Abigail's eyes. She couldn't just sit here. She had to figure out something.

Breathe in. Breathe out.

Breathe in. Breathe out.

Focus.

Her mind gradually registered more details.

She appeared to be in a rustic one-room cabin. A couch stretched across the wall to her right. A small kitchenette stood to her left.

A doorway stood in front of her, frayed beams of subtle light slinking around the edges.

Abigail stretched, and the splintered wood floor scratched her legs, which were covered only by thin black pajama bottoms—the ones she'd worn to sleep in.

When she'd gone to bed last night, she had no idea she would wake up to this.

Panic started to swirl inside her again, but she pushed it down.

What else, Abigail? Use your head.

Her mouth was dry, as if she hadn't had anything to drink for a while. Her jaw was sore. Tender.

Had someone hit her?

Another memory tried to slam into her mind, but she pushed it away.

She couldn't handle the horrid recollection. Not right now.

She was trained in public relations for crisis management. She'd told her clients that they needed to focus only on critical information and that every decision needed to be informed. That, and to never panic.

She needed to follow that advice now.

Focus. Informed. Without panic.

Drawing in a deep breath, she jerked her wrists. Her fingers felt both tingly and numb. Her skin was sore and bruised.

Still nothing happened.

She had to get out of here before that man came back.

Yes, *that man* . . . more tears pressed at her eyes.

She remembered him. Remembered how he'd punished her with his fists.

A rush of emotion rose from deep inside her until Abigail felt like she couldn't breathe. She'd never known a fear like this. Terror overpowered her, tried to consume her.

But she couldn't let it win.

She tugged her arms again, determined to loosen

the ropes. Instead, she flinched as her raw skin pulled against the sharp bristles.

She had to push through the pain, especially if it meant getting away.

As she tugged again, the door opened.

Abigail squinted, the light outside nearly blinding her.

Bile rose in her.

The person who'd arrived wasn't a rescuer coming to sweep her away from this horror.

Her tormentor was back.

"Please . . ." It was the first time Abigail had spoken since she'd awoken, and her voice sounded so scratchy she hardly recognized it.

The man's heavy footsteps stomped across the wooden floor until he stopped in front of her, his frame towering over her.

He was more of a shadow. The light behind him still blinded her. But, even if it didn't, the man wore all black, including a ski mask. She couldn't make out his features.

"Did you have a nice nap?" The man's voice sounded calm, almost soothing.

That deceitfulness only made him more evil.

Abigail stared at him, yanking at her binds once

more as desperation echoed in her survival-stricken mind. "Who are you?"

"That's not important." He stepped closer, still glowering over her.

Abigail shivered. His closeness was the last thing she wanted.

The man knelt in front of her and reached for her face, cradling her chin in his hand.

Abigail flinched, trying to scoot away from him. But there was nowhere to go—only the wall behind her.

"You are so beautiful, Abigail. But you probably already know that, don't you?"

"Don't touch me." Her voice quivered.

"Still feisty. Still not broken. I can't decide if you're like a wild horse or one in captivity."

She stared up, not saying anything.

The man examined her until he finally stood. "It's been fun. But this first part of our journey is over."

The first part? What did that mean?

"Let me go," Abigail croaked. "Please."

She'd had no intention of begging, but her instinct had other plans. Desperation made her feelings and actions clash inside her.

"I think I will," the man said.

Abigail swallowed hard, certain she hadn't understood him correctly. "You're going to . . . let me . . . go?"

"That's right." Satisfaction arched through the man's tone. "You need to give your father a message. Tell him if he doesn't do what he needs to do, there will be consequences. Consequences that will make our little rendezvous here seem like a walk in the park. Do you understand?"

A tremble raked through her at the thought of how much worse things might become. But all she cared about right now was getting away. She'd figure everything else out later.

"I understand."

The man knelt in front of her again and studied her face. Abigail wanted to look away. But she didn't. She needed to let him know she was strong. That she couldn't be bullied or tamed or broken.

"I'm going to cut the ropes around your wrists. If you try to come at me, I *will* use my knife on you. Do you understand?" His voice no longer held amusement as he pulled something from his pocket.

A knife glimmered in front of her, its blade pointy and sharp. "I understand."

"Good. Then I'm going to do you a favor. I'm going to leave you with this phone so you can call for help." He pulled a device from his pocket and set it in front of her. "Consider it my little favor to you."

She wasn't sure what that meant, but she nodded.

Then she waited, desperate to see if he'd stay true to his words or if he was tricking her.

He studied the six-inch blade of his knife for a minute.

Abigail's skin crawled as she wondered what he might do with it. What if he changed his mind and plunged it into her body?

More nausea rose in her.

He leaned closer until the blade shimmered mere centimeters in front of her face. The man's eyes . . . they were evil. He wouldn't give a second thought to hurting her.

Except that there was something else he wanted.

As he lifted the knife again, Abigail held her breath.

Please, Lord. Help me. Please, please, please!

He raised it as if he might plunge it into her chest.

A cry rose from the depths of her being, one she couldn't hold in.

As he lunged at her, she pressed her eyes shut and tucked her head, waiting for the pain.

Instead, one arm dropped to the floor.

The next instant, her other arm dropped.

Then, with a gloved hand, the man patted her cheek and muttered, "Good luck."

With those words, he rose and strode out the door, leaving it open behind him.

Freedom waited just ahead of her.

Yet Abigail couldn't bring herself to move. Fear held her in place.

This seemed too easy. What if the man was waiting out of sight? Maybe terrifying her with a surprise attack was just another part of his plan, and he got some kind of strange pleasure from it.

She rubbed her wrists. Rope still wrapped around the raw skin there. But at least her arms were free.

She squeezed back another image of what had transpired over the past twenty-four hours. Yet the memories hit her anyway. Images of the man's fists meeting her jaw. Of his hands going to her throat. Of the pleasure in his voice every time she cried out in pain.

She had to get away from him.

A motor roared to life outside.

Was that a . . . boat?

The sound became softer and softer until Abigail no longer heard it.

Finally, she dragged herself to her feet and staggered forward. As she did, she kicked something.

The cell phone.

She leaned down and picked it up before continuing to totter forward, unsteady on her feet as she rushed toward the door.

Maybe somebody was outside. Someone who could help her.

She could yell to get their attention. This was her chance to get away, to end this nightmare.

Yet when she stepped out the door onto the deck, water greeted her. Everywhere. On all four sides.

Her trouble was nowhere close to being over, she realized.

She had a feeling that was what this man had intended.

***

GRANT MATTHEWS LEANED FORWARD until his nose met his stallion's. "You're the bees knees, Howie. You got that? Don't let Nelly tell you any differently."

The horse snorted from the other side of the stall

door. Grant rubbed Howie's face one more time before stepping away. As he did, his phone rang.

He tilted his cowboy hat back as he glanced at the screen. He didn't recognize the number, but the area code was local. Though he considered not answering, an internal urging changed his mind.

He hit Talk and put the phone to his ear. "Hello?"

"Grant?" a shaky voice asked.

His neck muscles tensed when he heard the fear-stricken voice. "This is Grant. Who is this?"

"It's me. Abigail."

Abigail?

His muscles clenched even tighter as everything around him faded. Something was wrong.

"I need you." Her voice cracked. "Please. I need help."

Grant paced toward the door, ready to act. "Where are you?"

"I don't know. I think I'm in an old fishing cabin. On a small island. It's mostly marsh. Maybe somewhere on the Currituck Sound." A muffled cry sounded through the phone line.

"It's going to be okay, Abigail." Grant used his most soothing tone. "Can you look around? Tell me what you see?"

"I see . . . water. There's land in the distance. I

can't get to it. It's too far. The water's too deep. Too cold."

"What about the ground around you? Is it sandy?" Grant headed toward the Community Safety building next door. He needed to grab his truck keys. As soon as he had a location, he'd go find her.

"It's mostly marsh grass."

"How many buildings are on the property?"

"Just one. That's all there's room for. There's a small dock in the reeds. No boat." Her voice cracked. "Please, Grant. I didn't know who else to call."

"You did the right thing by calling me, Abigail." He stepped outside and sunlight flooded him. "Is there anybody else there with you?"

"Not anymore. The man . . . he left me here." Her voice cracked again.

Grant bristled. Had she been kidnapped? What had this man done to her? "I'm going to come get you, Abigail. Okay? You just hang in there."

"Do you even know where I am?"

"I'm going to try to ping your location from the phone. But I also know of five or six hunting and fishing cabins on the Currituck Sound. I'm going to send someone to check those also."

"Thank you, Grant. Thank you." Her voice broke as if she might be crying again.

The thought of anyone hurting her made anger surge through Grant's blood.

Abigail might come from one of the most awful families Grant had ever encountered, but Abigail herself was a gem, a diamond in the rough. She didn't deserve any of this.

That assessment had nothing to do with the fact that Grant was entirely attracted to the woman, even though he knew the two of them could never be together. Too many insurmountable obstacles stood in their way—obstacles that were ingrained in them, that would always remain, no matter what they did.

"Please don't hang up on me." Abigail's voice was just above a whisper.

"I won't. But I'm going to need to coordinate with a few other people, so I'm going to keep you on the line while I talk to them. Okay?"

"Okay. Thank you."

Grant gripped the phone as he charged into the station. He didn't have any time to waste if he wanted to help Abigail before the sun set . . . or before trouble returned.

CHAPTER TWO

ABIGAIL WAS SO COLD. She'd tried to stay on the small deck that jutted from the cabin, but the wind felt like daggers coming across the water. Instead, she slipped back inside the cottage, desperate for warmth.

January on Cape Corral could be like a tropical paradise or like a visit to an arctic village, depending on which direction the wind came from.

Today, it came from the north and brought with it a chill that made her shiver uncontrollably.

"Are you still with me, Abigail?" Grant's voice sounded through the phone line.

As soon as she heard his soothing tone, her shoulders softened. Grant would find her. Abigail knew he wouldn't give up until he did. That was the kind of person he was.

Still, she'd been trying to keep her distance from the man. She'd been daily reminding herself that flirting with any type of relationship with him would only lead to trouble.

But her body told her differently. Her heart sped every time Grant was near. Her mind played images of what it would be like to hold his hand. Even her soul seemed to curl with affection whenever his name was mentioned.

All those things, however, were to her detriment. The two of them were from different sides of the tracks, so to speak.

"Abigail?" Grant repeated.

"I'm here." Abigail pressed herself into the grimy wall near the door as she waited. She didn't want to venture any farther than she had to into the tiny cabin.

"The Coast Guard and the marine police are looking for you," Grant said. "I'm at the docks here in Cape Corral right now, and my friend is going to take me in his boat to help search. How confident are you that you're in the Currituck Sound?"

That was a good question. Five different sounds were located in the Outer Banks of North Carolina.

"I . . . I guess. I'm not sure. I just assumed the land across the water was Cape Corral. I could be wrong." As Abigail said the words, another deep chill captured her. This one wasn't from the elements, though. It was from the realization that she had no earthly idea where she was. She could be in Georgia, for all she knew.

"Do you hear anything?" Grant asked. "Have you seen any boaters?"

"No, it's been quiet. There's really nothing out here except water and a little sliver of land."

"Can you see the land on both sides of you or just one?"

"Just one. It must be to the east. The sun is going down on the other side."

"We're going to find you, Abigail. I need you to hold tight until we get there, okay?"

"Okay." But her voice wavered again.

When she'd stared at the phone, she hadn't known who to call. Grant was the first person who'd come to mind. He was law enforcement on the island, and, only a couple of weeks ago, he'd given her his phone number, just in case she ever needed it. She'd stared at it, pondering excuses to call him. In the process, she'd memorized it. Thank goodness.

Grant seemed like the most capable person who might be able to locate her.

Then again, her father had every resource at his disposal.

But he was up in New York for the week. He would be in meetings.

Abigail squeezed her eyes shut. Every time she heard Grant's voice, she knew she'd made the right decision. Every time she imagined his broad shoulders, steadfast gaze, and sincere smile, she knew he was someone she could depend on. There were very few people in her life she could say that about.

"Have you seen that new movie with Ryan Reynolds?"

She blanched, certain that she hadn't heard Grant correctly. "What?"

"It just came out in theaters a week or so ago. Have you seen it yet?"

"No . . ." Why in the world was Grant asking her about a movie right now?

"I heard it was pretty good."

As Grant said the words Abigail heard the hum of a boat motor over the phone line. If she had to guess, Grant was heading across the water now. With any luck, maybe she'd see him on the horizon.

Then again, maybe she shouldn't get her hopes up.

But what she really didn't want was for that horrible man to come back.

Her knees weakened and her head began to spin at the thought.

"There's a great seafood restaurant I've been wanting to try again down in Nags Head," Grant continued. "Maybe we can go there sometime. After we see the Ryan Reynolds movie together, of course."

She let her head fall against the wall, and a small smile tugged at her lips. "Are you choosing right now, of all times, to ask me out on a date, Grant Matthews?"

"Are you saying my timing is worse than a cat warming himself on a car engine?"

Despite her circumstances, she let out a little chuckle. Grant and his Grantisms. He was full of them.

It was just one more thing she liked about the man. She had a long list of his admirable qualities, however.

"Your timing is pretty awful," she told him. "And I know what you're doing. You're trying to distract me."

"Is it working?"

"Maybe a little."

"Good. Goal completed."

Abigail heard the smile in Grant's voice, even without seeing him.

She peered around the doorframe and spotted a boat in the distance. Hope leapt inside her. "Is that you?"

"Where?"

"Coming toward my cabin across the water?"

Grant paused for a split second. "I wish I could say it was, darling. But it's not me. What does the boat look like?"

Abigail's lungs tightened again as she stared at the vessel. "It's hard to say."

"Does it look like a fishing boat?"

She squinted, trying to get a better look. The boat looked too small to be Coast Guard but too fancy for a fisherman. "I . . . I don't know. But . . . I don't think so. Grant, what if it's that man? What if he's coming back?"

"Abigail, get away from the door." Grant's voice hardened with authority.

She closed the door, and darkness surrounded her again.

"Okay."

"Is there anything you can push in front of the door in case this guy returns?"

"There's . . . a couch."

"See if you can slide it in front."

"I'm going to put the phone down for a minute."

"I'll be right here when you get back."

With trembling hands, she lowered the phone to the floor. Then she grabbed the arm of the couch and pushed it. The furniture slid across the floor, effectively blocking the entry—for now. It wouldn't stop someone for long, but it would slow them down.

She snatched the phone back. "Done."

"Good girl. I'm going to stay on the phone with you. But don't open the door unless I tell you to. Do you understand?"

"I understand." She slipped into the corner and sank down, pulling her knees to her chest.

She couldn't bear the thought of that man coming back.

Because she knew the pain he'd bring with him if he did.

GRANT'S PULSE pounded harder in his ears as the cold wind hit his face. The boat charged forward, frigid water spraying him from the side of the boat, a reminder that winter was upon them.

His friend Wade Jessen stood behind the wheel. The man was a seasoned waterman, and Grant trusted him to navigate these waters, which could be tricky to pilot because of shallow areas with shifting sandbars.

As they charged across the Currituck Sound, Grant gripped the phone at his ear. He wanted to be there for Abigail if she needed him.

What if that person was coming back to hurt her again?

Concern spiked his blood at the thought.

One of his colleagues, Dash Fulton, was back at the station, trying to ping Abigail's phone. So far, he hadn't been successful. But they weren't giving up.

Abigail's image filled Grant's mind. The woman was slender and fit, a high school and college athlete. She had long, light-brown hair with sun-kissed streaks of gold running through the straight strands. Her eyes were brown but sometimes looked green in the sunlight. Her skin had a natural bronze to it.

She was soft-spoken and kind. She was also

intelligent and, at times, funny.

Basically, the woman had captured Grant's thoughts from the moment they'd first spoken after running into each other while jogging on the beach.

His throat tightened when he imagined her in trouble.

"Do you hear anything now?" he asked.

"It's quiet outside. No, wait. I can hear the boat." Her voice caught. "It's getting closer. It almost sounds like it . . . slowed down."

Grant gripped the phone tighter, turning from the wind so Abigail could hear him. "Do you have anything you can use to protect yourself with?"

"I can look."

"Do that." Just then, Grant's phone buzzed. "Hold on a second, Abigail. I'm getting a text message from Dash. Maybe he figured out your location."

Grant glanced at his screen. Dash *had* been able to ping Abigail's location.

Her signal was coming from somewhere on the north end of the Currituck Sound.

The signal wasn't strong enough to pinpoint her exact whereabouts, but at least Grant knew he was in the ballpark.

Gripping the side of the boat with one hand, he

put the phone back to his ear with his other. "Good news. I'm headed your way. I'm guessing we can be there in five minutes. Okay?"

"Okay."

Grant scanned the expanse of water in front of them, still looking for any indication they were getting closer to Abigail. "Do you still hear the other boat?"

"It definitely slowed down. I can barely hear it outside."

Grant's chest muscles tightened. He didn't like any of this. In fact, it made him sick to his stomach to think what Abigail might be going through—and what she had already been through.

Right now, he'd concentrate on saving her.

Once he knew Abigail was out of harm's way, then he'd comb through all those other details.

He motioned for Wade to call in an update to Levi Sutherland and Dillon McGrath, to let them know what was going on. Levi was the chief law enforcement officer on the island and Dillon the fire chief. The two of them needed to head this way too, just in case trouble arose. They also needed to let the Coast Guard and state police know the update.

Grant raised his binoculars and stared into the distance.

Was that a fishing cabin?

It looked like it.

Hope rose in him. Maybe that was where Abigail was. From what Grant could tell from a distance, the place fit the description.

As he got closer, Grant spotted a skiff cruising in the opposite direction from the island.

"Abigail, is the boat leaving right now?"

"It's hard to say for sure . . . but it almost sounds like it is. How do you know?"

His jaw hardened with determination. "I have you in my line of sight. I'm going to let Levi and Dillon go after this guy. But I'm going to come to you. Okay?" He said that word a lot, but he needed to know he was getting through to Abigail.

Shock and trauma could occur in situations like this. It wasn't just someone's physical state that Grant worried about. Their mental and emotional state was important as well.

"Thank you, Grant," Abigail practically whispered. "I knew I could count on you."

His jaw clenched again. He hoped he lived up to Abigail's expectations. He hoped he was at the right place right now.

But there were no certainties in this situation.

Right now, he only prayed for the best.

CHAPTER THREE

ABIGAIL COULDN'T CURL into the corner and act like a victim. If that man came back, she had to put up a fight. She only wished she could think more clearly.

Her captor . . . he must have drugged her. More than once.

The tenderness on her bicep seemed to indicate there was a needle mark there.

She couldn't focus on that now, though.

She glanced around the room again. What could she use as a weapon? There had to be something.

She pushed herself from the wall. Her legs trembled so badly she wondered if she could even move forward. But she forced herself.

A small cabinet stood in the corner. Maybe something was inside.

She scrambled toward it and opened the door.

A few old magazines were stacked inside. But nothing else.

No, wait.

She moved the periodicals aside. Something shiny rested beneath one of them.

An old steak knife! The utensil was dirty, and something reddish brown discolored the side of it.

Blood?

Abigail's heart leapt into her throat again. She couldn't think about that now.

Instead, she picked it up and slunk back toward the wall beside the door to wait. She would use this knife if she had to.

But she really hoped and prayed she didn't have to.

She rubbed her wrist again, her fingers slipping beneath that rope still wrapped around it. The raw skin there made her flinch.

Try as she might to keep the memories at bay, every time she closed her eyes, she imagined that man punching her. She pictured that look of evil in his gaze.

She couldn't go through that again.

Tears pressed at her eyelids.

"Abigail?" Grant's voice drifted through the phone line, reminding her that he hadn't ended their call.

"I'm here."

"We're coming up to a fishing cabin here. Can you hear a boat?"

She paused and listened. "Yes."

"That should be us. I'm going to dock and come to the front door. Wait until you hear me before you open it, okay?"

"Okay."

Maybe help really was almost here.

As Abigail gripped the phone, the device buzzed. She pulled it from her ear and glanced at the screen.

She'd gotten a text message . . .

As she read the words there, her blood went cold.

I can hear everything you're saying. I came back for more fun, but I can see help has arrived. Be free—for now. This isn't the end.

Cement seemed to fill her lungs.

Those words only confirmed one thing.

This man wasn't done with her yet. He had more planned, more ways of making her suffer.

Vomit rose in Abigail at the thought.

AS WADE PULLED CLOSER to the dock, Grant hopped off the boat and hurried up the trail leading to the rugged fishing cabin.

This had to be it, had to be the place where Abigail was being held.

He still gripped the phone, knowing he couldn't lose his connection with Abigail until he had eyes on her. "I'm coming up the steps now. Can you hear me?"

"I think so." But Abigail's voice sounded even raspier than before. Had something shaken her?

A moment later, he pounded on the door. "Abigail. It's me. Grant."

He waited to hear footsteps. Waited to hear Abigail scrambling toward the door. Waited to see for himself that she was okay.

But as he stepped forward, the deck boards beneath him creaked.

His spine straightened as he sensed something wasn't right.

As he looked down, the wood gave way.

The breath left his lungs as he began to fall.

He reached out and grabbed the side of the deck —the part of it that hadn't caved in.

As he did, the phone slipped from his hands and cascaded into the marsh grass below.

What had just happened? Were the boards rotted?

Grant didn't think so.

It was almost like he'd been set up.

But that didn't bring any comfort.

He glanced down, searching for his phone.

As he did, he spotted something sticking up from the marsh grass.

Several things, for that matter.

He squinted as he tried to get a better look.

Those were knives. Blades. A sword? Several daggers? Each stood straight up with the sharp blades pointing toward the sky.

There had to be at least twenty of the weapons directly below him.

Grant's muscles tightened.

Someone *had* set up a trap.

If he didn't pull himself back onto this deck, his body would plunge onto those blades—a fall he might not survive.

CHAPTER FOUR

ABIGAIL HEARD the commotion at the front door and tensed.

Her heart pounded harder. What was happening out there?

"Grant?" she called. "Grant? Are you there?"

There was no response. Was he okay?

Abigail called for him again, but there was nothing.

She couldn't just stand here.

Making a split-second decision, she pushed herself off the wall. She quickly shoved the couch out of the way and flung the door open.

She started to step onto the deck but froze.

A square section of the deck was gone, almost as if there had been a . . . trap door?

Grant gripped the edge of the opening with his fingertips.

Abigail fell to her knees as concern ricocheted through her. "Grant!"

His jaw tightened. "Give me a second."

Her eyes traveled below him, and she saw the marsh grass . . . along with . . . something else. Were those blades? Standing on end?

Her heart leapt into her throat again.

They were.

Someone had rigged this place.

Was this trap meant for her? Or for whoever might rescue her?

Abigail didn't know, but the situation seemed to grow worse by the moment.

She looked up as someone else ran up the steps —a man dressed in cowboy gear just like Grant's.

He must have driven the boat here. She'd overheard Grant say his name. What was it? Wade?

The man's eyes widened with alarm when he spotted her kneeling over the trap door.

Before either of them could attempt to help Grant, he swung his legs onto the other side of the opening and pulled himself up. He rolled onto the deck and sat up, drawing in a few deep breaths to compose himself.

Then all Grant's attention was on her. His gaze went from concern to horror. She must look terrible.

He quickly rose to his feet and reached for her. "Watch your step."

As she glanced at the open space in front of the door, her head swirled with dizziness. Grant gripped her hand and helped her over to where he stood. Her bare feet hit the rough wood.

As soon as she reached him, Grant pulled her into a bear hug. She melted in his embrace, grateful for his strong arms to hold her up right now. Now that she was safe, all her strength seemed to disappear.

Grant seemed to sense that also. In one quick motion, he scooped her off her feet and into his arms.

Abigail didn't try to stop him. Instead, her head fell limply against his thick chest.

"We need to get you out of here," Grant said. "Get you to help."

She wanted to argue. Wanted to say that they should sweep this place for clues. That they should chase after the man who'd done this.

But Grant knew what he was doing. She was safe with him.

He carried her down the steps, Wade following behind them.

Just as they reached the dock, another boat sped closer.

Levi waved to them. He was obviously trying to find the person who did this before he got away.

Abigail released her breath. Maybe hope was on the horizon after all.

Maybe.

AS THEY HEADED BACK toward Cape Corral, Grant wrapped his leather jacket around Abigail's shoulders.

She was a shivering mess.

But it wasn't even her trembles that bothered him the most.

It was seeing the ropes around her wrists and the red marks beneath them.

It was her bruised jaw and eye.

Her torn and bloody shirt.

The disheveled state of her normally neat hair.

Grant almost wouldn't have recognized Abigail if he didn't know it was her.

What had that man done to her?

Anger grew inside him at the thought.

Instead of dealing with that now, Grant wrapped an arm around her, trying to keep her warm until they could get back.

The sun had just about set, and the air was turning even cooler.

Once back on land, he'd drive Abigail to the island clinic so she could be seen by medical professionals.

When Grant knew she was okay, he'd get her statement and find out exactly what had happened.

But as he remembered those knives in the marsh, he realized that whomever they were dealing with was sinister. Common criminals didn't set traps like that.

Only sickos did.

In this case, a sicko who'd gotten hold of Abigail.

Grant fisted his hands again at the thought of it.

Finally, just as the sun set and cast yellow and orange streaks across the sky, they reached the docks of Cape Corral. The briny scent of the shore rose up around them, and eel grass layered what had once looked like a sandy beach.

Grant climbed out and helped Abigail onto the

dock's weathered planks. As she stood there, she looked like she might collapse.

Grant scooped Abigail into his arms again and carried her to the truck waiting in the distance.

Whoever did this would pay, Grant vowed.

He would make sure of that.

CHAPTER FIVE

ABIGAIL FORCED her eyes open as Grant gently set her on the front seat of his truck.

She wasn't sure what was happening to her. Was she going into shock? She barely felt able to function right now. Thank goodness for Grant.

He pulled the seat belt out and buckled it around her waist, careful to keep the jacket over her shoulders. As he did, Abigail caught a whiff of his leathery cologne. A moment of comfort filled her.

She loved that scent.

It brought her almost as much comfort as feeling Grant's strong muscles around her.

"We're going to get you all taken care of." Grant winked at her, the motion reassuring instead of flirty. "You just hold on for the ride."

Abigail had no doubt that his words were true.

He closed her door before running to the other side, hopping in the driver's seat, and cranking the engine. "I'm going to take you over to the clinic so you can be checked out."

Panic seized her and she sat up straighter. "No. I need to go back to my house."

Grant threw her a concerned look. "Abigail . . . I don't think that's a good idea."

"Please, don't take me to the clinic. I'll be fine. I just need to get home."

"Dr. Knightly is there. He should examine you."

"Nobody in this town wants to help a Ferguson." Her stark words spoke the truth. "Nobody but you, maybe."

Grant frowned. "That's not true. There may be a lot of animosity toward your family, but when it comes to things like this—"

She barely heard him. "I don't want anyone to see me like this. Everybody in town would probably be happy to know I was hurt. Maybe they'd even gloat about it."

"Abigail . . ." His voice trailed as he frowned at her again.

"You know it's true."

"I know that might be how it seems sometimes. I

know how things have been here on this island. But the locals are good people. None of them would wish you harm. Nor would any of them be happy to see you like this."

Abigail still didn't buy it. "I just want to go back to my house. You can't force me to go to the clinic, can you?"

He glanced at her another moment before sighing. "I suppose I can't force you to do anything. I just highly recommend it."

"Good." She nodded resolutely. "I need to go back to my house then. That's the best place for me to recover from this, not the island clinic."

Grant cast her one more skeptical glance.

Abigail ignored it. She had another challenge she was about to face when they got back to her place.

She was going to have to relive her nightmare. To rehash every detail with law enforcement.

She may be able to get out of going to the clinic, but she wasn't going to be able to escape giving her statement.

Dread pooled in her stomach as she anticipated dredging up the memories she wanted to forget.

GRANT PULLED beneath the huge oceanfront house Abigail and her family called home. After putting the truck in Park, he rushed around to help Abigail out.

She looked so frail, so injured. She might not even realize the extent of how beaten she appeared. Certainly, she'd go to the clinic if she did.

But Grant didn't want to push too hard.

Instead, he nodded toward the sprawling stairway in front of them. "Can you make it up the steps?"

Abigail lived with her family on the North Banks of the island. The area was also known by locals as "Ferguson territory."

Abigail's dad, Thomas Ferguson, had made lots of money in both the financial sector and the real estate market. Now, he wanted to turn their island into a resort area. But doing so would harm the wild horses that roamed these peaceful shores by taking away their habitat and causing more vehicular traffic.

A feud between locals and the Fergusons had arisen ever since the family moved here, but the tension had only grown worse over the past year. Just when those opposed to the resort seemed to make headway, it seemed like something else popped up and set them back again. No doubt, it would be a battle until the end.

There was a vast difference between the Fergusons and locals—and not just when it came to their plans for the island. The Fergusons' houses were new and big, with swimming pools and multiple levels filled with every convenience and luxury. The structures were practically mansions.

Locals, on the other hand, mostly had cottages that had been handed down from generation to generation. Most were small and humble but etched with memories and history.

Abigail was a Ferguson. Grant was considered more of a local, even though he'd only been on the island for six years. Those facts practically formed an ocean between them.

Grant watched as Abigail glanced up the stairway. The sharp wind coming off the ocean blew her hair into her face. She pulled his jacket closer and frowned.

Her eyelids looked even heavier than they had earlier. The woman was obviously exhausted. She'd been through so much.

Grant needed to find out exactly what those details held. He halfway dreaded hearing the truth, though. Abigail didn't deserve any of this.

"I think I can make it up the steps," she finally murmured. "Just hold on to me."

"Gladly."

Grant kept an arm around her waist as she started up the stairs toward the red front door at the top.

"Is anybody else here?" Grant was surprised no one had come out to greet her yet.

"My dad is on a business trip up in New York right now. My mom went with him."

"When are they going to be back?"

"They're supposed to be back next week," Abigail said. "I've got this place to myself. It's kind of been nice."

"What about your brother?"

"Johnny is in the Caribbean for another week. Everyone else has already returned up north for the winter. It's been like a ghost town around here."

Grant continued to help Abigail step by step as she navigated the flight of stairs up to the front door. The home had been built on stilts to combat potential floodwaters that occasionally arose on the island.

Finally, they reached the entry. Grant twisted the handle, and the door opened.

"I always lock it behind me," Abigail said softly.

Most likely, the man who'd abducted her had left it unlocked.

"Let me go first." Grant nudged Abigail behind him.

She nodded but remained close, as if she feared being too far away. The reaction was understandable.

As he closed the door behind them, the warmth of the house surrounded them. Everything in his line of sight appeared normal. He needed to check out the rest of the place to confirm that, though.

Before he could, he took a deep breath and a spicy, savory scent filled his nostrils. It almost smelled like someone was here . . . cooking dinner.

Abigail seemed to smell the aroma at the same time as Grant did, and she blanched as if a memory had hit her.

"I put some chili in the Crockpot last night." Abigail shook her head. "But I put the actual crock in the refrigerator so I could cook it today."

Grant's gaze darkened. "No one else is here, correct?"

"They shouldn't be."

"Stay there." Without waiting for a response, Grant strode toward the kitchen.

The Crockpot sat on the counter, a red light on in

front. He grabbed a napkin before placing it over the handle on top. As he pulled the lid off, he saw the ground beef, beans, and tomatoes.

But something else was nestled in the middle of it.

Was that a . . . heart?

CHAPTER SIX

ABIGAIL FELT her knees buckling as she pictured a heart mixed in with the chili in her Crockpot.

Before she hit the floor, Grant caught her elbow. "Let's get you a seat."

She didn't argue as he led her to the couch. She sank into the cushions, wishing she could disappear. Instead, she settled on pulling Grant's jacket closer.

"A heart?" She looked up at Grant, praying she'd misunderstood what he'd just told her.

His jaw stiffened as he studied her face. "That's what it looked like."

"Whose . . ." Nausea threatened to materialize, but she fought it. She couldn't finish her question.

"It's not necessarily human—it looks too small, in my opinion. Most likely, it's from a pig. After Levi wraps up his investigation at the fishing cabin, he's going to come by and check it out."

Abigail said nothing, only tried to control her breathing. This couldn't be happening . . . yet it was. Her troubles were far, far from over.

A heart had been placed in her chili. Someone had actually come into her house, left the ominous threat in her Crockpot, and plugged the device in.

That man had wanted Abigail—or someone investigating the case—to find it.

He had all of this planned out.

"I need to check out the rest of this place," Grant said. "You stay here. Okay?"

She nodded, though she didn't want Grant to leave her alone. She found so much comfort in his presence. Yet she knew she couldn't go with him either—her legs wouldn't hold her up.

Instead, she remained on the couch, her mind racing. As her nausea returned, Abigail's hand went to her stomach.

The last thing she wanted was to add throwing up to an already humiliating situation.

If she let her thoughts spiral, then her body would follow suit. She had to stay strong. There would be time for breaking down later. When managing a crisis, remaining as calm as possible was essential.

She'd told her clients that before. She needed to remember it for herself also.

As Grant strode back into the room, Abigail held her breath.

Had he found something else?

And, if so, was it equally as horrifying as that heart?

GRANT SAW the apprehension fill Abigail's gaze as he walked back into the room after checking her five thousand-square-foot house. It had been no small task, but he needed to be thorough—especially since he knew, without a doubt, that Abigail's attacker had been inside. He had to be certain the man hadn't left any more surprises.

"It's clear." Grant lowered himself onto the couch beside Abigail. "But we'll still need to dust for fingerprints or any other evidence that may have been left behind."

"Do you think this guy actually left anything to identify himself?"

He had to be honest. "Based on what I've seen so far, no. This guy seems to have put a lot of thought into his plan. But even the smartest criminals make mistakes."

Abigail nodded, as if still trying to process everything. She glanced down at her black pajama bottoms and knit shirt. "Can I . . . take a shower? Clean up?"

Grant sent her an apologetic frown. "It's better if you don't. We need to see if there's any evidence on you."

"Evidence? On me?" Her voice sounded even thinner than it had before.

"That's right. There could be a hair left on your clothing or some other fibers."

"He wore a full mask. I doubt it."

"Did you scratch your assailant? Could there be skin cells under your fingernails?"

"I . . . I don't think so. My hands were tied up."

Grant grimaced, hating the picture that formed in his mind. "I'll wait until Levi arrives with some evidence bags before we process . . ."

"Process *me*?" Her sullen gaze stared up at him.

"Before we document your injuries and look for evidence." Grant bit down, regretting his poor word choice.

Abigail crossed her arms and leaned back on the

couch, her gaze still entirely too hollow for comfort. "And now? What do we do now?"

"I need to get your statement. Are you up for that? I can grab some water for you. Your throat is probably dry."

She thought about it only a moment before nodding. "Let's just get this over with."

Grant released his breath.

Getting it over with sounded like a great idea.

CHAPTER SEVEN

DREAD POOLED in Abigail's stomach.

She knew she needed to tell Grant what had happened. But telling him meant remembering, and remembering was the last thing she desired. Grant sat on the couch beside her, patiently waiting for her to begin. If she had to tell someone, she wanted it to be him.

She pulled a weighted blanket over her lap. She hadn't thought she'd like it when her brother had gifted her with it at Christmas, but something about the heaviness between the fabric made her feel safe. She craved safety right now.

"May I see your arms?"

She sucked in a breath as more dread congealed in her stomach. Part of her didn't want

Grant to see how she'd been beaten. But she'd rather Grant take a look at her than anybody at the clinic.

After hesitating for a moment, she nodded.

Grant tenderly stretched her arm toward him. He ran his finger along the uninjured skin of her wrist.

"We should get this off you." He touched the ropes, and his jaw tightened.

"Don't you need to wait for Levi?"

He didn't answer her question. "You have bags in the kitchen?"

She told him where they were located. Grant returned with several a moment later. After taking a picture of the ropes, he gently cut them off using a pocketknife. He then put them in a bag.

When Grant finished, he gently pushed the hair from Abigail's forehead. He studied the bruises there before looking at her jaw.

Abigail could hardly breathe as she felt his touch. Her skin felt electrified. Her heart raced. Her lungs went still.

She might think after what had happened to her that being so close to Grant might frighten her. But Grant never scared her. He was like a gentle giant.

In other circumstances, no doubt he'd be cracking jokes and using his antiquated expressions to get smiles from people and lighten heavy moments.

But there was no sign of joking in him as he quietly said, "He did a number on you."

Abigail nodded, unsure what else there was to say.

She rubbed her hands over the gray blanket, still fighting nausea. "I really don't want to talk about this at all, even though I know I have to."

Grant squeezed her hand, his thick, strong fingers covering hers. "I know you don't. I know it's not going to be easy, Abigail. But we need to know the details of what happened if we want to catch this guy and bring him to justice."

Abigail knew his words were true. But that didn't calm her racing heart. "I don't suppose you've heard any updates from the people looking for the guy who did this to me, have you?"

"No, not yet. But I'm sure they'll inform me as soon as they know something."

She nodded, but her entire body felt burdened, from her feet all the way up to her eyelids, which wanted to close rather than lift the unseen weight pressing on them.

His eyes softened with tenderness. "I'm so sorry you went through this, Abigail."

A tear trickled from her eyes. She wanted to say thank you, but she couldn't. The words wouldn't leave her lips. All her emotions felt like they'd been boiling inside her, and now they wanted to overflow.

"Come here." Grant pulled her into his arms and held her.

Abigail wished she could stay like this and forget what happened.

If only life were that easy.

GRANT COULDN'T GET Abigail's bruises out of his mind. Couldn't stop thinking about what she'd endured. Couldn't erase the image of her fear.

And he hadn't even heard her story yet.

For now, he held her. Abigail had folded into his arms, and her tears wet his shirt. He didn't care.

The woman needed someone there for her. Her parents, in general, certainly weren't anxious to offer any support to their daughter—and Grant wondered how much compassion they would even show. The same with her brother.

One of the highlights of the past several months had been getting to know Abigail. She was nothing like Grant had thought she'd be. Nothing like the rest of her family, for that matter.

That was a good thing.

Her family was haughty and selfish. They made no attempts to befriend people outside their circle. But looking at Abigail, it was clear she was different. That she saw other people as equals. That her wealth didn't define her.

Grant waited until she pulled away from his embrace. When he saw her red-rimmed eyes, he reached for the Kleenex box on the table beside him. Abigail took several tissues and dabbed beneath her eyes, trying to dry them.

Even in her disheveled state, the woman was still beautiful and fascinating. She'd captured his thoughts for a long time.

Right now, she was clearly on the verge of breaking.

"I'm ready." Her voice sounded shaky as she said the words.

"Take your time."

She nodded and dabbed her eyes again. "It all seems like a blur, to be honest. I hardly know where to start."

"Just start at the beginning."

She nodded and drew in a quivering breath.

"Last night . . . I went to bed about eleven. No one is home but me right now. I was sleeping pretty soundly when I thought I heard something. I jostled awake, but, as soon as I did, a hand covered my mouth. Someone was in my bedroom."

Grant's heart pounded in his chest as he imagined the horror of what Abigail had been through.

"It was a man in a black mask." Abigail's expression pulled tight. "He wore all black so I couldn't see any of his features."

"What did he do?"

"He told me he'd been planning for this moment for a long time. Then he injected me with something. I blacked out."

"What happened next?"

"I woke up in that fishing cabin. My arms were tied to the wall. The man was there, and he told me my family needed to pay. That's when he started beating me. I went in and out of consciousness."

Grant's throat tightened. The thought of somebody doing this to Abigail—to any innocent human being—made fury rush through him.

"I guess that went on for most of the night." She pressed her lips together, more moisture welling in her gaze. "So much of it is hard to remember. Maybe my mind blocked it out. Anyway, the last time when

I woke up, he told me he was going to free me, but . . ."

"But what?" Grant held his breath as he waited to hear what else she had to say.

More moisture filled her gaze. "He told me to give my father a message—that if he doesn't do what he needs to do there will be consequences that make what happened today feel like nothing. Then he said this wasn't the end and to be free—for now."

Grant's back straightened. He didn't like the sound of that. His muscles threaded with protectiveness.

Whether Abigail wanted him to or not, Grant was going to need to talk to her father. Because it looked like what had happened was a direct result of Thomas Ferguson's actions.

That was just one more reason not to like the man.

Grant already had a long list.

CHAPTER EIGHT

ABIGAIL THOUGHT she'd feel worse after sharing her story with Grant. Instead, she felt a rush of relief. She hadn't realized that holding the truth inside had caused her to feel so burdened.

Grant felt like a rock, which was strange considering the fact that Abigail didn't know him that well. But she couldn't deny the connection they'd shared from the moment they had first met while jogging. Seeing him was one of the highlights of her day.

"Abigail, did you recognize the man?" Grant asked.

"No, he had a mask on the whole time."

"What about the man's voice?" Grant leaned closer, his intense gaze on her. "Did it sound familiar?"

She shook her head as the man's words replayed in her mind. *This isn't the end.* "I wish it did. I wish there was something to help me identify him. But nothing about him seemed familiar."

"It sounds like this man hurt you as a way of getting revenge on your father. Was that your impression?"

She squeezed her eyes shut, trying to push down any resentment she felt toward her father. She'd tried to believe the best in him, but deep inside she knew he'd done shady deals under the guise of business.

Now she was the one paying the price.

"That's definitely how it sounded," she finally said.

"I know these are hard questions, but they're timely," Grant continued. "Do you know why he might want revenge on your father?"

"There are too many reasons to count. My father has made a lot of enemies. That probably doesn't come as a surprise to you."

Grant shifted, graceful enough not to agree. "Have you heard any chatter in the house? Did you hear anyone talking about anything you think might have provoked this?"

Abigail thought about his question a moment

before shaking her head. A lot of things had been talked about. After a while, she'd tried to tune most of those discussions out.

She'd rather live her life in peace than immerse herself in her father's business dealings.

Now she realized she should have listened more closely. "I wish I could tell you something that would help. But I really don't know. I try to stay out of my father's business as much as I can. Life is simpler that way."

"I understand," Grant said quietly. "I *will* need to talk to your father about this, though. Do you want me to be the one to tell him what happened?"

A moment of panic rushed through her at the thought. Hearing this news from someone other than Abigail might cause more hard feelings between her father and locals. "I don't think that would be a good idea. I'll tell him. I just need a moment to collect myself."

"Of course. Whatever you need. Can I get you something to drink or eat?"

"I'm okay. I don't think I can hold anything down."

All she really wanted was to disappear, to recover.

Yet she didn't want to be alone.

Before she could say anything else, a knock sounded at the door.

Abigail jumped back, pushing herself into the couch.

Who was here now?

What if more trouble had arrived?

GRANT HEARD the knock and tensed. Most likely, it was Levi. But he had to use the utmost caution right now.

"You weren't expecting anyone tonight, were you?" he asked Abigail.

She shook her head. "No, no one."

"Stay there." He wouldn't put anything past this guy, and he needed to be certain he wasn't putting Abigail into a dangerous situation.

He rose to his feet and walked toward the door. One of his hands went to his gun as he approached.

When he peered out the side window, Grant released his breath. He opened the door, and Levi strode into the foyer. As the head of the island's Forestry Service Division, he was the lead law enforcement officer. Though he was only a year older than Grant, Levi had taken over the position when his dad retired, and he did a fine job of keeping peace on the island.

"It didn't take you as long as I thought," Grant said.

Levi put his bag down—one that contained his crime scene kit and, hopefully, a new temporary phone for Grant. "I left Dash there to finish up."

"Anything?"

Levi's grim expression said it all. "Nothing that would lead us to finding out who he could be, or where he could've gone."

Disappointment pressed on Grant. He'd desperately hoped this guy would be apprehended and Abigail would be safe. Even though it hadn't happened yet, it would. Grant promised himself that.

Levi nodded toward Abigail and lowered his voice. "How is she doing?"

Grant glanced back at her also as she stared forlornly at the wall, her eyes glazed. "She's shaken, but she refuses to go to the clinic."

"I'm glad we found her when we did. We examined that booby trap, and those knives would have meant death for anyone who fell on them."

Grant's jaw tightened as he vividly remembered seeing the blades hidden in the marsh grass. "That's what I thought. Someone executed that very precisely. But what I don't understand is how the trap door was triggered when it was. Abigail stood in that area earlier, and it didn't open on her."

"There was a camera outside the door. That guy was watching. When he saw you standing there, he must have pulled some type of electronic trigger that released the booby trap."

Grant's mental picture of this man continued to grow darker and darker. "That sounds awfully advanced for a criminal around here."

Levi's eyes gleamed in agreement. "My thoughts exactly. This person knew what he was doing and put a lot of planning into this."

"I don't like the sound of that."

"Neither do I. Not at all." Levi narrowed his gaze, his entire body tense as if he was preparing himself for a long fight for justice. The man was good at his job, despite the obstacles that had been thrown at them recently. Grant had no doubt he would see this through.

"Do we know who owns that cabin where we found Abigail?" Grant asked.

"That's actually what I came here to talk to you about."

Grant braced himself. Whatever Levi was about to share, it didn't sound like good news.

"The fishing cabin belongs to a man named Merle Miller, who lives down in Corolla. I asked if authorities there would send an officer to talk to him. When the officer got there, he discovered that Merle was dead."

Grant's breath caught. "What happened?"

"He'd been shot. But there was a note left at his place."

"What did the note say?"

Levi rubbed his jaw before saying, "That this was just the beginning."

CHAPTER NINE

ABIGAIL'S HEAD spun as Grant and Levi told her what they'd discovered about the fishing cabin.

Levi pulled up a photo on his phone and showed it to her. "Do you recognize this man?"

She studied the picture of Merle Miller, the man who'd owned the fishing cabin. He appeared to be in his sixties with a long salt-and-pepper beard and a wrinkled, hooded gaze.

"I wish I could tell you something that would help you, but I've never seen that man before." Abigail pushed back the feeling that she was disappointing them with her answer. The truth was the truth.

"So you don't believe he was anybody that your father knew?" Levi asked.

"I'm not always around for my father's business dealings, but they are usually with businesspeople. Merle very well could have been a businessman, but from looking at the photo of him, he doesn't strike me as that type."

"He runs a bait and tackle shop down south," Levi said.

"Does he own any land here on Cape Corral?" Grant asked Levi.

Abigail knew what he was getting at. Property here on the island had been a point of contention between her family and the locals for a long time. Unfortunately, frictions had only grown worse lately.

"As far as we can tell, Miller only owned the little cottage in Corolla where we found his body and the fishing cabin," Levi said. "We'll keep looking, and maybe we can discover some type of connection. In the meantime, I'm going to need to talk to your father."

She nodded. Grant had told her the same, and Abigail knew it was coming. She just dreaded speaking to her father about this situation. She dreaded his reaction. The two of them had never had a great relationship, but it had felt especially strained lately.

"I can call him," Abigail said. "I'd like to tell him

what happened first before you talk to him, if that's okay."

"Of course," Levi said.

After a moment of hesitation, she took Levi's phone. She wasn't sure where her own was at this moment. She dialed her father's number and waited for him to answer.

To her surprise, a woman's voice came over the line.

"Yvonne?" Abigail said.

"Abigail! Your father is in a meeting so he asked me to take any calls for him. I wasn't expecting to hear from you."

Yvonne was one of her father's secretaries. The woman didn't live here on the island, but instead was based out of the company's home office in New York.

"I know my father is a busy man, but there's something urgent that I really need to speak with him about." Abigail gripped the phone as apprehension continued to build in her.

"Urgent enough to interrupt him from a business deal?"

Abigail swallowed hard. She'd been in this world her whole life, so Yvonne's words didn't surprise her.

When it came to her father, work was always his number one priority.

"Yes, it's that urgent," she said. "I wouldn't have called otherwise."

Yvonne paused for a second before saying, "Let me go see what he says. Hold please."

The sickly feeling continued to grow in Abigail's stomach as she waited. What if her father refused to talk to her? It wouldn't entirely surprise her.

Finally, a moment later, her dad's gruff voice came on the line. "This better be important. You know how vital this deal is."

Grant, who sat next to her on the couch, scooted closer. No doubt he could read her body language right now. Maybe he could even hear bits and pieces of their conversation.

"Father," Abigail started. "I don't know how else to say this, so I'm just going to come right out with it. I was abducted and beaten by a masked man. But the police managed to find me before . . ." She couldn't finish her sentence.

Her father didn't say anything for a moment before muttering, "What?" Disbelief stretched through his voice.

"This man who did this is trying to send you a message," Abigail continued. "He wants me to be sure to tell you that he's not done yet and that you should do what you need to do. Do you know why somebody might have done this, Father?"

"No! Of course not. I would never put myself in a situation where I thought my little girl might get hurt."

For some reason, guilt pressed on her at his words. Maybe he wasn't trying to make her feel guilty, yet somehow, she did. That was usually the way things worked with her father.

"The police want to talk to you," she said. "They need to find this guy."

"You're talking about those police there on Cape Corral? We'd have better luck with the police in Mayberry."

Her guilt turned to irritation. "Dad, these guys are heroes. They saved me today."

"Of course, they did, honey. I don't mean to sound harsh. I just want the best for my little girl."

She ground her teeth, trying to remain patient. "When are you coming home?"

He hesitated before saying, "I have five more days of meetings here."

Abigail's heart sank. That meant she had five more days of staying here alone. She supposed that part of her had hoped her father might rush home in her time of need.

She should have known better.

"I understand," she finally said.

"Is that Grant guy one of the police officers with you?"

"You mean Officer Matthews?"

"Yes, him."

Abigail glanced at Grant. "Yes, he is."

"I want to talk to him."

Why would her father want to talk specifically to Grant? Abigail knew better than to question him.

"Hold on." She handed the phone to Grant and frowned. "He'd like a word."

She braced herself for whatever was about to unfold.

GRANT FELT himself bristle as he took the phone from Abigail.

Though he needed to talk to Thomas Ferguson about this investigation, he had a feeling that wasn't why Thomas Ferguson wanted to talk to him. Knowing the man the way he did, Grant halfway expected him to reprimand him or blame this whole incident on Cape Corral.

He braced himself as he answered. "Hello, Mr. Ferguson."

"My daughter told me what happened." Mr. Ferguson's voice sounded brisk and professional. "I need to hire you."

"Hire me?" Had Grant heard him correctly?

"That's right. Abigail is going to need full-time protection."

"Of course, law enforcement around here will do everything that we can—"

"I need more than just some second-string local law enforcement moseying around about their duties. I want someone to act as her bodyguard. I want it to be you. She trusts you. I can tell by the way she talks about you."

His words made Grant's heart pound a little faster. So Abigail had been talking about him? That was something to think about at another time.

"Unfortunately, I also have a full-time job to do," Grant said.

"I'm sure you can work out something. On your off time, I want you to be with her until her mother and I can come back to town."

Grant didn't like the man's demanding tone. "When will that be?"

"Five days."

Another rush of anger went through Grant. How could this man not come back and be with his daughter in her time of need?

Another part of him wasn't surprised. The reaction seemed pretty typical for the man. Grant had hoped that maybe he'd misjudged him but apparently not.

"Well?" Mr. Ferguson said. "What's your answer?"

Grant glanced at Abigail, at her wide eyes. Something about them had always softened his heart. "I will do anything and everything I can to keep your daughter safe."

"That's what I wanted to hear. You're hired. We can talk about money later. I'm willing to pay whatever you need."

"This isn't about money—"

"Whatever your currency is, consider it done. I need you to keep my daughter safe and find the person who did this to her."

Grant's back muscles tightened as the conversation drew on. "That's precisely what I wanted to talk to you about. I need to find out who might have a vendetta against you."

Mr. Ferguson laughed, the sound dry and unconcerned. "Who doesn't? How much time do you have for me to make this list?"

"I'll take all the time it requires. If that's what needs to happen in order to find the person who did this to your daughter, then that's what we'll do."

Grant would sacrifice anything if it meant keeping Abigail safe.

CHAPTER TEN

WHEN HE WAS YOUNG, he'd been eating a French fry when he accidentally bit his finger. He'd been so hungry he hardly noticed.

Then the blood came.

And he realized he'd let his hunger control him.

He'd vowed to never let that happen again.

Desperation would *not* be a part of his vocabulary, and he'd worked hard to ensure that he was never again a slave to his needs.

Now he needed to continue with his plan.

Tormenting Abigail Ferguson was actually more fun than he'd thought. He'd assumed he might feel bad. But he'd found a surprising delight in each of his actions—and he found even more delight in the future actions he had planned.

A smile curled his lips.

He lingered in a dark house across the street from where Abigail stayed now. From his window, he had the perfect view of everything going on.

He had lots of views of Abigail, even ones she couldn't possibly know about.

He'd learned to disappear, to not be seen. But he'd also learned how to be in control.

His grin grew wider.

He was just disappointed that Grant Matthews hadn't been able to fully experience that booby trap he'd set up earlier. He'd been so looking forward to watching the man fall to his death.

Oh well. He had other ways of toying with the Fergusons and any who associated with them.

And in the end, Thomas Ferguson would capitulate to whatever he wanted.

He would ensure that.

He stepped away from the window and walked to his goodie bag.

It was time to prepare the next part of his plan.

CHAPTER ELEVEN

AN HOUR LATER, Levi left with the crock of chili. He'd been on the phone with Abigail's father, trying to make a list of people who might possibly want to harm Abigail.

After the two of them had finished talking, Levi looked at the feed from the security camera outside the house and then collected the cell phone the man had left for Abigail.

Meanwhile, Grant pulled on some gloves he'd taken from a bag Levi brought and gently took her hand to scrape beneath the fingernails. He took pictures. Collected evidence.

Everything he did was professional and done with delicacy.

Abigail appreciated it.

Afterward, she took a shower and cleaned herself up. When she caught a glimpse of herself in the mirror, more nausea clutched her stomach. The bruises . . . the dirt . . . her bloodshot eyes. They didn't form a pretty picture.

In fact, Abigail almost didn't recognize herself.

The only comfort she found was in knowing that Grant was here watching out for her. If he wasn't, Abigail didn't know what she'd do. Disappearing into a corner or a closet sounded tempting. But she knew she wouldn't even be safe there.

Someone had gotten into her home with ghostly precision, not leaving a trace behind. She hadn't heard a thing. There was no evidence the lock had been picked.

Those realizations left her feeling unsettled, to say the least.

Finally, she put on some clean leggings and an oversized sweatshirt. Instead of drying her hair, she pulled it into a bun high atop her head. She was halfway tempted to add some makeup to conceal her bruises. But it didn't matter. Grant had already seen them.

As she stepped back into the living room, a twinge of anticipation captured her.

Even though she and Grant had been talking for

a while, something felt different about being alone with Grant now. The thought brought her a strange sense of excitement in the middle of all this chaos.

Abigail felt almost shy as Grant glanced up and watched her walk into the room. She rubbed her neck as she remembered how beaten and swollen her face looked. Thank goodness, he hadn't seen her abdomen and the bruises that were there also.

Grant rose from the couch. His hands went to his waist as he observed her a minute. All six-plus feet of his well-sculpted body seemed tense with concern.

"Do you feel better?" His voice sounded strained.

"I do. Did I miss anything while I was gone? Any updates?"

"No, nothing new. But we have a lot of people working on this. We just need more time."

She sat on one end of the couch. "I know you do. Thank you."

He sat near her, close enough that their knees brushed. "How are you holding up? It's been a long day for you. Do you need to get some rest?"

"It's kind of strange how I can feel exhausted and wide awake at the same time. I guess I feel too jittery to try to sleep."

"But maybe you should just close your eyes for a

few minutes." As he said the words, he pulled her feet into his lap. Just the act of feeling Grant touch her somehow made her feel better, made her feel more connected and not so alone.

If it wasn't for Grant, Abigail would be by herself right now.

Part of that was her father's doing.

Her father . . . who'd tried to hire Grant.

Was that why Grant was being so nice right now?

At that thought, Abigail sat up straighter and pulled her feet down to the floor. "I don't want you to feel like you have to stay here and guard me out of obligation. I know my father can be a bully at times and—"

Grant's hand went to her knee before he murmured, "Even if he hadn't asked me, I wasn't going to leave you here alone tonight."

She studied his face and saw the sincerity there. But still, this was a lot to ask of anyone. "Are you sure?"

"I'm positive. You shouldn't be alone after something like this."

"Well, I appreciate it. I just don't want to put you out. I don't expect your life to revolve around my troubles—"

Grant leaned closer. "Abigail, you never have to feel that way with me. Understand?"

Heat rose on her cheeks. For her entire life, she'd never had anybody look at her like that or sound that sincere. Her parents had always thrown her off on nannies or sent her to boarding school. The one person in her life she'd ever really felt cared about her was Lucia, a live-in nanny who'd worked for the family for four years. Lucia had listened to Abigail when nobody else had.

Until she'd suddenly quit.

Abigail never heard from her again after that.

Abigail tried not to feel sorry for herself in that poor little rich girl manner. But being near Grant now reminded her of everything she'd been missing.

He pulled her feet back into his lap and patted her leg. "You just take it easy. We'll worry about the rest of this later."

She nodded and rested her head back on the couch. Taking it easy sounded nice . . . but also impossible.

TEN MINUTES after Abigail closed her eyes, Grant watched as her breathing smoothed out and her chest rose and fell in even motions.

Finally, she was asleep.

That was a good thing. Her body needed to recover from the trauma it had endured.

Grant didn't plan on waking her. He'd let her snooze here on the couch, and, if he needed to, he'd rest on the couch perpendicular to this one.

But Grant didn't intend on resting. Not with everything that was going on.

There were too many disturbing details he needed to attend to first.

Mr. Ferguson had made a list of potential enemies. As Grant stared at those names, he knew his team had their work cut out for them.

There were thirty-three people on here.

These were just the ones he'd rattled off quickly. Apparently, Mr. Ferguson might add others later.

At the top of the list was a man named Richard Rodriquez, who used to work maintenance for the Fergusons here in Cape Corral. He'd quit in a fit of anger over his pay.

Six people total had been fired from Ferguson's company.

Also on the list were a former business partner, an old neighbor in New York, and a brother who'd fought with him about a family inheritance.

The list went on from there.

Grant shook his head. He couldn't even imagine having this many enemies. He supposed when a person was in a position of power, that's what happened.

Mr. Ferguson had started in the finance world and moved into real estate. He had properties all over the world, but his newest focus was Cape Corral. Ferguson Enterprises had all the resources anyone could ever dream about—and that made them even more of a threat.

Grant started with the first name on Thomas Ferguson's list and began researching the people. Levi had dropped off Grant's laptop earlier, so he used that now.

The first several people he looked into led to no answers.

But when Grant went to Richard Rodriquez's social media page, a photo caught his eye. The picture appeared to be from a party the Fergusons had hosted here in Cape Corral.

In one of the candid shots, the camera's focus was on Thomas Ferguson. But in the background,

Grant saw Richard standing there, shooting a death glare toward Abigail.

What was that about?

Grant had no idea, but he knew who he'd be looking into first thing in the morning.

CHAPTER TWELVE

ABIGAIL SHOT upright on the couch, a cold sweat covering her skin.

Was she back in that fishing cabin? Had the man grabbed her again, causing her to black out first so she wouldn't remember?

She jerked her hands in front of her.

They weren't bound.

She released a quick breath. But her relief was short-lived. Darkness still surrounded her, the blackness adding confusion to her already jumbled thoughts.

"Hey," a soft voice said. "It's me. Grant."

Abigail's gaze jerked toward the voice. It was familiar. It was close.

That really was Grant, wasn't it?

As her eyes adjusted to the darkness, she saw she'd fallen asleep in her living room. Grant knelt in front of her as she tried to gain her bearings.

His hands went to her knees as he locked gazes with her. "Everything is okay. I'm right here. No one else."

She nearly collapsed against the couch with relief. For a moment, she was back at that horrible place with that horrible man. Fear had nearly crippled her.

She never wanted to relive that again. The thought of it made her want to curl into a ball and never leave this house.

Grant moved to the couch beside her and pulled her into his strong arms. She nearly melted there. The strength Abigail found in his embrace was such a gift.

But she knew better than to get used to it. Grant had been a good friend, but they could never be anything more. Too many obstacles stood between them. But it would be nice, just for a moment, to ignore those barriers, to pretend they didn't exist.

"You were sleeping hard," Grant murmured.

"I must have been." She brushed several stray hairs away from her face, still blinking sleep from her gaze. "When I woke up, I had no idea where I was and . . ."

"I know."

She sniffed, a new aroma filling her nostrils. "Are you . . . cooking?"

"I hope you don't mind, but I figured you could eat something when you woke up. I don't cook much, but I *can* make a mean omelet."

"That sounds great. I just thought . . ." Her eyes drifted to the windows, and she saw the blackout shades were drawn. Her father had trouble sleeping if there was even a hint of light. "I thought it was the middle of the night."

"It's almost seven. I wanted to let you sleep for as long as possible. You didn't get to sleep until close to two a.m."

"That's nice of you." But Abigail made no effort to move. Instead, she rested her head against Grant's chest, relishing the steady rhythm of his heart pounding against her cheek.

She had to get a grip. She couldn't keep acting like this. Yet she had been through a horrific ordeal. She'd be a fool if she thought she could just bounce back.

Abigail pulled away from Grant's embrace and

let out a deep breath. "Food does sound good. So does coffee."

"As you wish." He stood and offered his hand.

After a moment of reluctance, she slipped her hand into Grant's and stood. He didn't let go as they walked into the kitchen.

"Have a seat." He nodded to a chair at the table.

Abigail sat down as directed. As she did, Grant brought her a cup of coffee before going back to the stove to work on her omelet, whistling as he cracked an egg into a bowl.

He wore jeans and a white T-shirt that showed his defined muscles. His fit physique made Abigail's throat feel a little dryer. Yet it was more than his looks that caught her attention. She admired how confident the man was—not just in the kitchen, but with life in general. He always seemed to take things in stride.

Abigail wished she felt the same way. But with her family, she was always walking on eggshells. Pleasing them felt like an impossible task. Now when she needed them the most, they weren't even there for her.

She shouldn't be surprised.

But the knowledge didn't take away her hurt.

Still, she knew she needed to make some

changes in her life. Yesterday's events had confirmed that.

GRANT SET a plate with a Southwest omelet in front of Abigail before seating himself across from her. "Eat up."

He observed her a moment as she stared at the plate.

She still looked so pale, so shaken. He couldn't blame her. The woman had been through a lot, and it would take time to heal.

But the paleness of her skin only made her bruises and cuts more noticeable. Every time Grant saw them, anger rose inside him, each instance feeling fresh.

"Aren't you eating?" Abigail nodded to the empty space on the table in front of him.

"I already grabbed something to eat. I've been up a while."

She eyed him, not bothering to hide her scrutiny. "Did you sleep at all last night?"

He shrugged, knowing there was no use in lying to her. "Not really."

"I hope you didn't stay up on my account . . ."

"I stayed up because I wanted to."

She gave him another skeptical glance before taking a bite of her omelet. "This is good."

"If I give up my job with the Forestry Division, maybe I'll give Mrs. Minnie a run for her money." He winked.

Mrs. Minnie owned The Screen Porch Café, the one and only restaurant on the island. She was known as the island cook and was determined not to let anyone take her place—the seventy-year-old would fight someone with a spatula if they tried.

"I have never eaten there, but I hear the crab cakes are amazing," Abigail said before taking another bite of her food.

"They are. I'll have to take you there sometime."

Her smile slipped. "I'm sure that wouldn't go over well."

"Why wouldn't it?" Grant watched Abigail's expression, curious about her thoughts on the matter.

She tilted her head, making it clear that no answer was necessary. Grant already knew the answer to that question. She didn't think any of the locals would appreciate her presence in one of their establishments, not when considering what a troublemaker her father had been.

"Give it a chance one day," Grant said. "Not now. But when you're ready."

She offered a grateful smile as if appreciating his understanding. Grant let her take a few more bites before he ventured into the next subject.

He cleared his throat. "I feel like I should know the answer to this question, especially considering how many times we've talked in the past. But do you need to call anyone about work?"

"I work for my father, so I think I'll be okay."

Grant observed her for a moment. "What exactly do you do?"

Her cheeks reddened. "I studied business and communications at Princeton. Afterward, I worked for a PR firm out of New York. Then two years ago, my father asked if I'd join the family business."

"So you do PR for him?"

She almost seemed to squirm. "I suppose."

"Why don't you sound confident?" He felt sure there was something she wasn't saying.

"I actually do crisis management."

Grant let that thought settle over him before repeating, "Crisis management?"

Abigail nodded. "That's right. When companies are getting bad PR, they'll often call firms that specialize in making their image more positive."

Grant drew in a deep breath. "You're the one who's been trying to paint this resort in a positive light? Who got those magazines to do stories on it and the other positive press?"

"Grant, I know how that sounds—"

"I didn't think you wanted the resort." How could he have read her so wrong?

"Sometimes, it's not about what I want, but about what I was hired to do."

He shook his head, unsure if he liked hearing about this side of her. It was more fun when they talked about jogging and playing lacrosse and eating exotic foods. He understood job responsibilities . . . but Abigail was working for her family—and her family stood for everything that Grant opposed.

"Grant . . ." Her eyes pleaded with him.

This wasn't the time to get into it. He knew that. Plus, he needed to process what he'd just learned.

"Maybe we should change the subject." He shifted in his seat. "Besides, we need to talk about this case."

"Of course." She wiped her mouth, her features still tense.

"What do you know about Richard Rodriguez?"

Abigail froze, her eyes widening. "My father's former maintenance man?"

Grant nodded.

She seemed to think about it a moment before shaking her head. "I . . . I don't know what to say. He worked for the family for probably ten years, basically from the time we moved to Cape Corral."

"Did he have any hard feelings toward you or anyone else in the family?"

"You could say that. He said he wasn't getting paid enough, and he quit."

"Did anything preface that?"

She shrugged. "You'd have to ask my dad, really. I try to stay out of things."

Grant leaned closer. "What about you? Did you ever have any problems with Richard?"

Abigail's eyes widened even more. "Me?"

"That's right. You."

She started to shake her head but stopped herself. After a long sigh, she said, "There was one time . . ."

CHAPTER THIRTEEN

ABIGAIL WISHED she could eat more of the omelet, but her appetite was gone. Instead, she placed her hands on her lap and leaned back in the kitchen chair as past events battered her thoughts.

She looked up at Grant, who waited for her to explain.

"Richard is probably seven years older than I am," she started. "I always try to be nice to anybody working for my family. The good Lord knows the rest of my family isn't. But I want the people my family hires to know that I see them, that they're valuable and not modern-day servants. But I think Richard took my attention the wrong way and thought I was interested in him."

"You weren't interested in him?" Grant took a sip

of coffee as he waited for her answer.

"No, he wasn't my type."

"Was it because you couldn't see yourself with someone of his social standing?"

"His social standing?" Her eyes widened at the implication. "You mean, because he was a maintenance worker?"

Grant nodded. "I suppose."

"No, of course not. That doesn't matter to me. Money doesn't matter to me. Did you think it did?" Abigail tried not to sound offended, even though she was.

Grant frowned apologetically, even though he'd clearly wanted to know the answer to that question. "I . . . I wasn't sure."

She pushed her plate away, disappointed by his answer. "I thought you knew me better than that."

He leaned toward her, not bothering to hide the curiosity in his gaze. "You grew up wealthy. If you married someone without money—"

"My father would probably disown me." Abigail couldn't deny the implication. Grant was absolutely correct.

"Exactly. You'd have to give up your wealth. Would you be willing to do that?" Grant studied her face, undoubtedly watching for her reaction.

Abigail raised her chin. "To be honest, I'm kind of insulted that you're asking. But, yes, I'd give up money to build a life with someone I loved. I've seen money destroy people. Destroy families. I don't understand why people worship it so much and act like it will end all their problems. Wealth just gives you a different set of issues."

"Sometimes it's because people want what they don't have or they think money makes them powerful."

"I suppose." She shrugged.

"And I'm sorry to insult you. I don't want to assume anything, either way I look at it."

She rubbed the side of her coffee mug as she gathered her thoughts. "Anyway, I wasn't interested in Richard. One day, I ran into him out on the beach. We talked for a few minutes before he tried to kiss me. I had to tell him I didn't like him in that way. He didn't take it well."

"I can imagine. Nobody wants to hear that."

"After that, he stopped talking to me. He gave me looks just like that one in the picture you showed me. It was like he resented me for not being interested. A couple of weeks later, he quit."

"Did you ever see him again?"

"No, I didn't. He left the island." Abigail locked

gazes with Grant. "I want to find the person who did this to me more than anyone. But, honestly, I don't think Richard is our guy."

"Why not?"

"I don't know." She shook her head, trying to find the right words. "I guess the man who abducted me didn't strike me as Richard. I've been around Richard enough that I think I'd recognize his voice or his build or his mannerisms. I just don't think it was him."

"Good to know."

Abigail stared across the table at Grant, trying to read his body language. "What now?"

He stood and grabbed her plate. "Now, I'm going to clean up breakfast. Afterward, we're going to try to figure out who did this to you."

Was it too much to hope that they might actually find some answers?

Abigail didn't know. She also didn't know if things would ever feel normal unless the person who did this to her was behind bars.

AS GRANT CLEANED THE KITCHEN, Abigail got dressed.

He wished the two of them could stay in this house all day, that he could keep her tucked away where no one could get to her.

But did any such place really exist? Grant knew the answer was no, especially when he considered there weren't any marks indicating the locks had been tampered with. How had that man who'd abducted Abigail gotten inside?

The only thing that made sense was that he'd had a key.

Grant didn't like the thought of that. He added changing the locks to his To Do List for today.

Abigail had insisted that she go to the station with him. Though Grant vowed he wouldn't let her out of his sight or put her in any situations where she might be at risk, he knew if he wanted to find the person who did this, he wouldn't simply be able to stay in this house all the time.

When Abigail stepped from her room, Grant sucked in a breath.

She'd fixed her hair and put on some makeup. She wore a cable-knit sweater with skinny jeans and boots.

The woman was a sight to behold.

She always was.

Her makeup nearly covered all the bruises on

her face, so much that someone might not even be able to tell they were there.

Her eyes also contained a familiar brightness. Maybe getting fixed up and looking halfway normal made her feel better.

"I'm ready to go when you are," she announced.

Grant pulled himself together and stopped staring at her long enough to nod. "Great. We'll head to the station. Levi or Dash will probably want to go over a few things with you. While one of them does that, I'll get cleaned up. I have a change of clothes in my locker there."

"Will we come back here tonight?"

"We'll go wherever you'll be safe. I'm going to change these locks later today. But either way, I assure you that you'll be taken care of."

She nodded. As she did, Grant flung his bag over his shoulder and stepped toward the door.

He wanted to check things out before he escorted Abigail from the house.

But as soon as he stepped onto the deck, his gaze caught sight of something waiting just outside the door.

Shackles.

A note had been left beneath the iron handcuffs.

A note that read, **The best is yet to come.**

CHAPTER FOURTEEN

ABIGAIL COULDN'T STOP STARING at the shackles. Trembles overtook her body as she remembered glancing out the door and seeing them.

Grant took her elbow and led her back to the couch. His temporary burner phone was already at his ear as he reported what he'd found, most likely to Levi.

As soon as he ended the call, he turned to her. "I need to look at that security footage from outside your house."

"Of course."

They walked down the hallway to a small room with a desk full of monitors. Levi had used this space yesterday, and Grant seemed to know how to operate the equipment as well.

He found the correct video and slowed the footage down. Though darkness filled the screen, Grant leaned closer, almost like he saw something.

Abigail leaned closer. The time at the bottom of the screen read 3:30 a.m.

A man in black practically slithered onto the front porch. His actions were fluid and easy—almost like he was an expert at remaining light on his feet.

Her head began to spin when she saw the man stare into the camera. He was clearly letting everyone know he was there.

The look in his eyes was pure malice.

This man was playing a deadly game . . . and Abigail's life was at stake.

GRANT TOOK Abigail to the station to get her away from the house for a while.

Meanwhile, Levi was at her place collecting evidence.

This nightmare wasn't ending—nor was there a finish line in sight. Whoever was behind these acts was determined to make Abigail suffer for as long as possible—just as he'd indicated when he released her.

Abigail paused outside the Community Safety building and stared at the front door, a frown tugging at her lips. She pulled her arms over her chest and opened her mouth before shutting it again.

Grant leaned closer. "What's wrong?"

Her gaze flickered toward him. "I'm a Ferguson. That's what's wrong."

Realization dawned on him. Of course. Grant should have seen this coming.

But Abigail had nothing to worry about.

"The guys inside . . . they're going to love you," Grant said. "Trust me."

She flashed a grateful smile. "Thanks, Grant. I do love your optimism."

But Grant could tell Abigail still didn't quite believe him.

He prayed for the best as he ushered her inside and introduced her to everyone. Then he left her in Dash's office while he went to clean himself up in the locker room area.

When Grant returned, Dash was examining the phone the man had left with Abigail at the fishing cabin. Based on the serious looks on their faces, whatever they were watching on the screen wasn't good.

"What's going on?" Grant crossed to the other side of the desk for a better look.

Dash's frown said it all. "There were some videos left on the phone."

"Videos of what?" But even as he said the words, Grant already had a good idea of the content.

Abigail stood, her limbs trembling again, as she moved away from the desk. "I don't need to see them again."

With one more glance at her, Grant lowered himself in the seat beside Dash and watched the video.

His throat went dry at what he saw.

The man who'd abducted Abigail had taken a video after he'd tied her up and held her hostage. In the footage, Abigail was obviously passed out. The man laughed in the background as he muttered, "There are some things money can't buy—things like peace of mind."

Hearing the man's words made Grant feel sick to his stomach.

Before the reel ended, the man turned the phone around until his masked face filled the screen.

Grant held his breath, unsure if he really wanted to see or hear what was going to happen next.

Even in the dark, the man's eyes appeared to be smiling.

"One person has the power to stop all of this," the man crooned. "The question is: will he?"

CHAPTER FIFTEEN

EVERYTHING FELT like a blur around Abigail. The hits wouldn't stop coming, and that was exactly the way this man wanted it. He wanted to let her know he was still in control.

She crossed her arms, suddenly feeling weaker than she'd like. She craved a safe haven—but she had none. Not even her home was a shelter for her anymore. As much as she'd like to think that Grant could be her rock, she reminded herself that those thoughts were foolish.

If she dated Grant, she'd essentially ruin his good standing in the community. Her family would probably disown her. The sacrifice just seemed like so much . . . for both of them. She could never ask Grant to give up everything for her, and she was quite certain he'd say the same. Still, she knew someone like Grant would come around only once in a lifetime.

Dash cleared his throat and held up the phone he'd been examining. "I'm going to keep looking for more evidence. The device is a burner, so we probably can't trace it back to the person who bought it. But maybe there are other clues that were left."

Grant nodded from his position behind the desk. "That sounds good. Any other updates I need to know about?"

Dash shook his head. "No, but we're doing everything we can to find this guy."

Abigail wished that made her feel better, but it didn't. The man who'd abducted her, who taunted her . . . he felt untouchable.

After all, he'd been able to slip in and out of her house. He'd left a clue on the porch, even though Grant had been right inside her house. The man had even thought ahead enough to leave a message on the phone, knowing they'd eventually find it. It seemed as if every base was covered.

That seemed to confirm to Abigail that whoever was behind this was fairly intelligent. Of course, she already knew that. After all, the man had left a booby trap and cameras to monitor the situation at the fishing cabin.

She only wished she had an inkling who he might be.

But she had no idea.

Even though Grant had mentioned Richard, Abigail had a hard time believing he'd be responsible for something like this. These crimes didn't fit his personality or what she knew about him.

But apparently, her dad had left a list of about thirty other people to check out. Hopefully, the police were whittling down those names to several who might be more likely suspects.

"Would you like to go out to the stable with me to check on the horses?" Grant's voice cut into her thoughts.

Abigail felt herself brighten at the suggestion. She'd always loved horses. She'd even owned several while growing up. Something about horses and the beach made her feel like all her dreams were coming true.

On good days, at least.

"I would love to," she finally said.

"Great." Grant nodded toward the door. "Let's go."

Maybe seeing these animals would help her forget her problems for a minute.

But Abigail knew that her troubles would still be there, taunting her, and that her captor was just waiting to strike again.

***

"SO THIS IS YOUR HORSE?"

Grant watched as Abigail rubbed the side of Howdy Doody's—also known as Howie's—face.

Something about seeing the two of them together warmed his heart. He could so easily envision Abigail fitting into his life.

But could *she*?

Even though Abigail said that money wasn't important, could someone who grew up with such privilege walk away from that kind of wealth? Certain things had to be ingrained in her, right?

That's the way it had been with Charlotte, at least. Grant had thought the two of them would get married one day. But Charlotte's family hadn't approved of Grant. They said he'd never make enough money to support a family and had pushed him to try to get a job in finance instead of law enforcement.

But that wasn't where Grant's heart was. The last thing he wanted was an office job where he'd be behind a desk all day.

Eventually, Charlotte had called things off. Looking back now, four years later, Grant could see it was for the best.

Yet, in some ways, Grant's life seemed to be a string of rejections. First, his father. Then his mother. Then Charlotte.

Though he tried not to let things get to him, those facts remained in the back of his mind, standing as a battleground full of reminders each time he faced the possibility of getting attached— and, by default, hurt.

He reached toward Howdy Doody and rubbed the other side of his horse's face, coming back into the moment. "He's the best horse I've ever owned. Smart as a whip, faster than lightning, and as spirited as a choir of ghouls at a Halloween singalong."

"He certainly is pretty."

"He prefers to think of himself as handsome." Grant winked.

A smile stretched across Abigail's face, the exact reaction he'd been going for. Rewards like that made Grant feel good for the rest of the day.

Abigail pulled her hand back and leaned against

the wood door of the stable. "You seem right at home here on Cape Corral. Yet you didn't even grow up on the island, did you?"

Grant readjusted his cowboy hat, grateful for the safe subject. "I'm an Alabama boy. But this place is where I was assigned when I went to work for the Forestry Division. It was one of the best placements I ever got."

"I'm glad you like it here."

"How about you? You're a New York girl."

"I'm *officially* a New York girl, but, honestly, my family spent most of our time down in Miami. My dad did real estate development deals down there before we moved here." Abigail's cheeks flushed at the statement, almost as if she hadn't wanted to bring the subject up.

Grant could see why. It was definitely a topic of disdain here on the island.

"How do you like Cape Corral?" Grant asked, curious about her take on this place.

"I love it." Abigail's eyes lit. "I've always wanted to live in a small town and have never considered myself much of a city girl. When you couple this place with the wild horses and the beach and cowboys . . . I'm pretty much smitten."

Grant raised his eyebrows. "You have a thing for cowboys, huh?"

"I always have. My mom used to always chastise me about my fantasies with them. Not *fantasy* fantasies." Her cheeks reddened. "But I did have a bit of a crush on the idea of a cowboy when I was a teenager. Fergusons do not have crushes on cowboys."

Grant laughed. "That's good to know."

Abigail studied him a moment, and Grant didn't complain. The woman could study him all day, for all he cared. Whatever made her happy.

"You know, the two of us have talked a lot when we run into each other on our jogs on the beach," she said.

Grant didn't tell her, but it was never a matter of running into each other. He pretty much knew when Abigail ran every day, and he'd made certain to run that same direction so their paths could cross.

"But, despite that, I really don't know that much about you," Abigail said. "I mean, other than how much you love certain movies and music from the eighties, that you played lacrosse in college, and that you love axe throwing. Maybe lassoing too."

"Lassoing is great, but Dillon thinks he's the king of it ever since he lassoed that helicopter not long ago. Now he thinks the sun comes up just to hear him crow."

She smiled again. "I remember hearing about that lassoing incident. You are all certainly fascinating."

"As are you."

Her cheeks reddened a little more. She turned back to Howdy Doody, rubbing the horse's face again. "Can I ask a personal question?"

"You, Abigail Ferguson, can ask me anything you want."

A wave of heat rose in her before she cleared her throat and plunged into her question. "Have you ever been married?"

"No, I haven't. I came close. But in the end . . . the two of us just weren't meant to be. We had different goals for the future, and we couldn't seem to reconcile those things."

She leaned closer to Howdy Doody. "That can be problematic."

"Yes, it can be. How about you?"

She shrugged, her attention still focused on Grant's stallion. "I was engaged two years ago to a man named Stephen, but I called it off. Best choice I ever made."

"Why'd you call it off?"

"Basically because, when I envisioned my future, it looked exactly like my family expected it to look, but not the way I wanted it to look. My fiancé was just like my father. If I married him, I was going to continue this cycle that I've seen in my life. I couldn't let that happen."

Grant's curiosity spiked. "What kind of cycle is that?"

Abigail shrugged and turned back toward Grant, but her gaze appeared heavier now. "My father is very controlling. He likes things to go his way. It seems that no matter what I do, I never live up to his expectations. I went to Princeton even, thinking that getting into an Ivy League school would satisfy him. But it didn't. Nothing ever does."

Grant rubbed his lips together. There was so much he wanted to say to Abigail about how she deserved so much more.

But before he could say anything, someone new walked into the stable.

Dash strode toward them, the hard look in his eyes making it clear he had an update.

Grant braced himself for whatever the news might be.

CHAPTER SIXTEEN

ABIGAIL FELT tension threading between her muscles as she waited to hear what Dash had learned.

"I just got off the phone with the police down in Corolla," Dash said. "They've been looking into the death of Merle Miller. Apparently, a neighbor saw a man outside Merle's house two days ago. We cross-referenced this man's name with this case and got a hit."

"Who is it?" Abigail rushed, knowing they had no obligation to tell her. But she hoped that they would.

"The man's name is Dawson Bergen," Dash said.

She gasped at the familiar name. "Dawson? He . . . used to be one of my father's business associates."

Dash shot a finger gun at her, letting her know she had hit the bull's eye, so to speak. "Exactly."

Abigail squeezed the skin between her eyes, trying to make sense of that news. "I don't understand. Why would Dawson be behind this?"

"That's what I was hoping to talk to you about," Dash said. "What do you remember about Dawson and your father?"

"They started off in business together." Abigail tried to remember any important details, but her thoughts felt muddied. "About a year and a half ago, Dawson decided to branch out and start his own company. I don't remember a lot of conflict around his parting. My father didn't seem upset about it, nor did Dawson."

"Do you have any idea why Dawson might be talking to Merle?" Grant asked.

Abigail continued to search her thoughts, trying to uncover a memory that would help. But she couldn't. She had no clue. Except . . . she mentally shook her head. That detail couldn't be important . . . could it? She needed to think about it another moment.

"I wish I could tell you something useful," she said. "I really do. But Dawson is in finance. I can't imagine why he'd be talking to Merle, of all people. You said Merle owned a tackle shop, right?"

"That's correct." Grant's jaw tightened as if in thought. "A connection between those two men makes about as much sense as the Hatfields and McCoys having a picnic together."

"The police in Corolla are trying to track Dawson down right now so they can talk to him," Dash said.

"There is one other thing that I guess I should share, just in case it's important." Abigail cleared her throat, dreading what she was about to say. But she couldn't keep this detail inside. What if it was important? "Dawson's son is the man that I was engaged to."

Grant's eyes widened. "Well, butter my biscuit . . . was Dawson upset when you broke off the engagement?"

Abigail drew in a deep breath. "I . . . I don't know. He caught me alone and begged me to reconsider my relationship with his son. Said I was good for Stephen and that our union would do good things for the company."

"What a statement."

She nodded. "Tell me about it. But once I told Dawson that I was done, he didn't push it. Once it was done, it was done."

But a bad feeling still brewed inside Abigail's gut.

GRANT SPENT the rest of the afternoon looking into more names from the list Thomas Ferguson had given them. He could easily eliminate several people because of alibis.

But three names rose to the top of the list.

Maintenance man Richard Rodriquez was one of them, even though Abigail said she didn't think he was behind this.

The second person was Henry Berkshire, a former neighbor of the Ferguson family in New York. The man actually had a criminal record for an assault. When Grant had called the man's home, his wife had said that she hadn't seen him in a few days and that he claimed to be on a hunting trip.

And the third person was Dawson Bergen. The Corolla police were still trying to track him down, but so far no one had found him.

As Grant glanced over at Abigail, he saw that her eyelids were getting heavy. She sat in the seat across from him in the office, rifling through some old magazines.

Maybe bringing her here had been too much for

her. She needed her rest after what had happened to her.

Grant stood from his desk. "How about if I get you back to the house?"

Abigail looked up from her magazine and frowned. "Don't feel like you need to go back for my sake."

"I think I can do anything else I need to do from the house. What do you say?"

She set the magazine aside and yawned. "If you don't mind, I suppose that does sound nice. I am a little tired."

Grant nodded toward the door. "Let's go then. How about we get a crab cake sandwich on the way?"

Her gaze lifted before quickly darkening again. "That sounds nice but . . ."

"But what?"

"I'm not sure I'm in the right frame of mind to deal with people's stares."

Grant wanted to argue with Abigail, but she might have a point. Plus, he could understand her reluctance. "Another time then. Honestly, I could probably order some and have Uber Stan deliver them to the house."

Uber Stan was what locals called a man on the

island who drove people around. Since the bridge had washed out, people had to take a boat over. Once they got here, they usually needed transportation—and that's where Stan came in.

They walked outside to his truck.

But Grant couldn't stop thinking about what might happen next. The pattern set by the man who'd abducted Abigail indicated there were more tricks up his sleeve. This guy liked to drop dangerous surprises, and, most likely, he even got a kick out of it.

Grant helped Abigail into the truck before climbing in himself and starting down one of the sandy roads that cut through the island. The truck bumped along as they traveled. The sun was already beginning to sink in the sky, casting soothing shades of pink around them.

They passed several harems of horses—one group grazed in a field and the others were on the dunes. Grant told her the horses' names and their stories. One mare had three babies in the past several years. Three of the mares were known as the Mean Girls by Grant and the gang. Apparently, that group of horses thought highly of themselves.

Grant went into storyteller mode and used his most animated tone to tell her about life here on the island. He was rewarded with smiles and follow-up questions.

Finally, they pulled up to Abigail's place. "I'd like you to stay in the truck for a moment with the doors locked, okay?"

Her eyes widened, but she nodded, seeming to understand. "Of course."

After Grant was certain Abigail had locked the doors, he headed up the stairs to her place. He wanted to check out the inside of the place and give it a brief perusal before letting her go inside.

He didn't want any more surprises—no more pig hearts or shackles or mysterious messages.

He had a new lock kit with him, and he'd replace the exterior door hardware this evening.

Five minutes later, Grant was back outside.

He hadn't seen anything suspicious.

Instead of walking right inside, Abigail paused beside his truck. She closed her eyes, inhaling a deep breath of air.

"It's surprisingly nice out here, especially considering it's the middle of winter," she said.

"It is."

Silence stretched, and Grant let her have a moment. He sensed that she needed it.

"I can't believe my parents didn't come back."

Her voice sounded grim and laced with hurt when she finally spoke.

Grant's lungs froze. He wondered if she'd bring up that topic today. He hadn't wanted to broach the subject and stir up more bad memories for her. "I'm sorry they haven't been there for you."

"I shouldn't be surprised, yet part of me is." She frowned as she leaned against the truck, the wind tugging at her hair.

In the distance, Grant heard the waves crashing and seagulls squawking. The salty scent of the ocean rose around them, normally soothing. But could anything soothe Abigail at a time like this?

"Family should be there for you," Grant finally said.

She offered a fleeting smile. "Yes, they should. Thank you for being there. You've been a real life-saver, to say the least."

Grant's heart warmed. "I reckon I'm good for something."

"You're good for a lot of things."

His grin faded as he realized just how fond of this woman he was becoming.

How did he tell her he'd be more than happy to be there for her . . . forever?

CHAPTER SEVENTEEN

ABIGAIL WASN'T in a hurry to go inside her house. Even though she felt desperate for rest, being outside and getting some fresh air helped her feel like she could breathe.

She and Grant shared a moment of quiet as they turned and stared at the beach. Several pieces of driftwood had washed up on shore and looked like nature's artwork on the sand. The sight of the drift-wood and the waves and soaring seagulls was always soothing, no matter what was going on in her life.

It was one more reason she loved this place.

Abigail stole a glance at Grant as he stared over the water. His cowboy hat remained on top of his head, creating a handsome profile, especially when coupled with his white T-shirt, fitted jeans, and brown leather jacket.

"Why do you talk with those antiquated expressions?" Abigail finally asked the question she'd been thinking about since she met the man. "I can't figure you out."

Grant crossed his arms and leaned against the truck, seeming to take her question in stride. "My dad jumped ship before I was born, and my mom decided that being a parent was too much for her. She left when I was three, and I went to live with my grandmother."

Understanding passed through Abigail—understanding because she'd experienced her own grief, only in different ways.

"I'm sorry," Abigail said softly.

"No need to be sorry. My grandmother was a great woman. We didn't have much, but she loved me. I grew up in Alabama, and my grandmother was the biggest character—always telling stories and entertaining people. To answer your question, it only seemed natural that I picked up on some of her Southernisms."

"That makes sense."

Grant continued to stare at the ocean, occasionally adjusting his hat or sending a quick glance at

Abigail. "When I went away to college, I tried to change my vocabulary so I could seem more sophisticated. Then I realized I shouldn't change something that's not broken. Those expressions are part of my heritage. They connect me with my grandmother."

Abigail's heart warmed at his explanation. His story only added another layer of affection for a man who was already easy to love. "They add a lot of color to life and make me smile."

"And that's just one more reason why I shouldn't change. Life needs more color sometimes, don't you think?" He winked.

She turned toward him, something inside her aching to get closer to him. To be near enough to feel his warmth. To catch a whiff of his spicy cologne.

"You definitely shouldn't change, Grant Matthews," she finally murmured. "You're a breath of fresh air."

"Well, I think you're finer than a frog hair split four ways." As he grinned, their eyes caught.

How did Abigail express to him just how much of an impression he'd had on her? Even when they weren't together, she thought about him all the time. She looked forward to running into him while she jogged. Those encounters were one of the main reasons she kept doing it every day.

She had never met anybody quite like him.

But she also knew that there was no way her family would approve of her dating a local—especially a local who was so involved in the community and a main proponent against her father's plans to build a resort.

Not that it really mattered. She was a grown woman, and she could do what she wanted to do.

But her family would make everything more complicated.

Besides, would Grant even want to be with someone whose last name was Ferguson? All her father had done was create a headache for everybody here on this island. She wouldn't be able to blame Grant if he wanted nothing to do with her.

But why did her heart feel so differently?

AS GRANT STARED down at Abigail, he saw something swirling in her eyes. Gratitude? Maybe. But there was more there, wasn't there? Or was he just imagining things?

He couldn't be sure.

He only knew that Abigail was as pretty as a peach and as sweet as a plum in the height of picking season.

Whenever the two of them were together, he was keenly aware of her presence. Of her every move. Of everything she looked at.

Grant couldn't seem to stop himself from touching her. From holding her hand as he helped her from the truck. From giving her hugs when she needed comfort. From checking out her ankle when she'd hurt it once while jogging.

The two of them had been flirting with romance for a long time.

But something held him back.

Maybe a *lot* of things held him back.

Family was important to people, and Grant knew what a stressor it would be for Abigail if she ever tried to bring someone like Grant home to meet her parents.

Not only that, but certain people on the island would feel like they couldn't trust Grant if he dated a Ferguson. Some people would feel like his job was compromised, even though he knew it wouldn't be.

But having trust in their law enforcement officers was a serious concern.

Could Grant maintain his position of authority on this island and date somebody like Abigail?

He wasn't sure. Perhaps that was what held him back all these months of getting to know her.

"You ready to get inside?" he finally asked, his throat burning with emotion.

She nodded, her gaze lingering on him a moment longer. "I guess we should."

Grant took her hand into his and started to lead her to the front door.

But, before they reached the stairs, a loud *boom* cracked the air.

Pieces of wood and metal flew through the air around them, mixed with bursts of fire and heat.

Grant threw himself over Abigail, using his body to shield hers.

Her home had just exploded, he realized.

CHAPTER EIGHTEEN

ABIGAIL'S EARS RANG. Her heart raced. Sweat covered her brow.

What just happened?

The cinders, smoke, and fumes in the air only confirmed what she already knew.

Her house had just blown up.

Blown up? How could that be?

She tried to raise her head, but Grant's body still shielded her. They'd hit the sandy ground together as the world seemed to explode around them. Her world, at least.

For a brief moment, despair tried to grip her. Then she remembered that Grant had put himself between her and this blaze. He'd been willing to absorb any of the hurt that might come.

Her heart filled with gratitude.

Maybe not all was lost. The important things—the important possibilities—were right here.

Grant was right here.

But Abigail didn't have time to fully revel in the realization.

Grant pushed himself off her, but only slightly. "Are you okay?"

She squinted. Was that what he'd said? Her ears were ringing.

She nodded anyway. Without his body weight on her, she drew in a deep breath. But the humming in her ears made her feel off-balance.

Grant rose to his feet and helped Abigail stand. She brushed the sand off as she staggered away from the fire.

A cry caught in her throat at what she saw.

Her home was destroyed.

Grant wrapped an arm around her before pulling out his phone. He called the incident in and assured her that firefighters would be here soon.

But Abigail knew that there was no saving her house. It couldn't be recovered from something like this.

Abigail didn't need to know what had happened to know who had done this.

Her abductor.

He was trying to send another message.

Trying to get her father's attention.

Abducting Abigail hadn't done the trick.

Would blowing up this place?

Acid swirled in her stomach.

She had the feeling that the answer to that question was yes.

TWO HOURS LATER, most of the flames had been extinguished. But it would take much longer before they could go inside the house. Not that Grant needed to investigate to know what happened. The man who had attacked Abigail had clearly set a bomb in the house.

Where had the bomb been? Grant had searched the place and hadn't seen anything. Then again, he hadn't opened every cabinet or closet door. For all he knew, the device could have been planted in a trash can or even beneath the house.

Grant was just grateful that Abigail hadn't been any closer when the bomb detonated.

If that had been the case, then neither of them would be standing here right now.

But the person responsible had known that, hadn't he?

Grant figured the guy was too smart to be anywhere close by. But he must have set up a camera somewhere. He must have been keeping an eye on them and waited for just the right moment to detonate the bomb.

He glanced around, looking at the other houses nearby. Dash and Levi had gone to check out the structures, to check for any cameras or other devices left there. He felt certain that something would be found.

This man was playing a sick, twisted game. Everybody here on the island was going to have to be on the ball if they were going to get through this.

He couldn't imagine what other lengths this man might go through to get Thomas Ferguson's attention, however.

In fact, Grant was going to need to call the man himself. The two of them needed to have a long talk.

As he glanced over at Abigail, Grant saw she was still shaking—as anyone in her shoes would be.

He slipped an arm around her shoulders, wishing he could take all her pain away.

He couldn't do that.

But he could find the person responsible and stop him.

CHAPTER NINETEEN

"WHERE ARE WE GOING?" Abigail asked as she and Grant rode away from the remains of her house and into the darkness.

"I thought about letting you stay at the inn, but I'd feel better if you stayed at my place. Are you okay with that?" Grant glanced at her, as if trying to catch her reaction.

She twisted her hands together in her lap, a swell of nerves rising in her. Staying with Grant sounded entirely better than staying anywhere without him.

But still . . . "I don't want to impose."

"It's not imposing at all. In fact, Emmy's already bringing a few things over for you."

Emmy Sutherland seemed like a real sweetheart on the few occasions Abigail had spoken with her.

She ran the inn, which was located by the station where Grant worked.

"That's awfully nice of her."

Grant shrugged. "That's kind of what she does."

Abigail sat quietly, reality still washing over her in mind-numbing waves. No matter how she tried to frame it, she couldn't wrap her thoughts around everything.

"I can't believe my house exploded," she murmured, the event replaying in a continuous reel in her mind.

"None of us can. To say that things are escalating would be an understatement."

As much as she'd like to dwell on today's events, she knew she needed to look ahead, to focus on solutions instead of problems. It was one of the few good pieces of advice her father had passed on to her.

"What next?" she asked.

"When we get to my place, I'd like to call your dad. I need to have a long talk with him."

Abigail nodded. She'd figured that was coming. Talking to her father was the next logical step.

But she didn't look forward to the outcome of that conversation.

"This guy's always one step ahead of us, isn't he?"

Abigail's voice came out softer than she'd intended. But the stress of everything was beginning to fray at the fibers of her being.

Grant glanced her way again, shadows lining his handsome face. "It does appear that way. But we'll catch up with him. I can promise you that."

"This man . . . he waited for us to get close enough to send a message, didn't he?"

Grant nodded, his expression unmistakably solemn even in the twilight. "He did. This guy . . . he's calculating. If we'd just been a few more steps closer . . ."

Abigail glanced down at her hands, which still laced together in frenzied movement in her lap. "What's it going to take to stop him?"

"I don't know." Grant's voice sounded grim but not defeated. "But we'll figure out something."

GRANT FELT a rush of nerves as he opened the door to his cottage. He wasn't normally one to feel self-conscious about things. But his place was tiny in comparison to Abigail's.

He knew she'd said that money wasn't important

to her. But what would she think when she saw just how humble his abode was?

"Go on in." Grant held the door open.

Abigail stepped inside and glanced around.

Grant paused beside her, trying to see his place as Abigail might be seeing it right now.

His home definitely wasn't fancy. The walls were plain white. Most of the furniture was dark-brown leather. Emmy had come over once and helped him pick out a nice rug for the middle of the space. Otherwise, the walls were decorated with some old photos left here by a previous owner.

"This is my castle," Grant said. "Albeit a small and humble one."

"It's really nice." Abigail nodded as she glanced around. "And cozy."

She was being kind. Grant didn't have to be a genius to figure that out. But it was best that Abigail saw him for who he really was. Pretending to be someone he wasn't or being in denial over their differences would get them nowhere.

He placed his hand on the small of her back and led her toward the hallway in the distance. "Let me show you where you can stay tonight."

She nodded as if she were fine with that, but Grant felt her trembling beneath his touch.

He opened the door to a guest bedroom and ushered her inside. Hopefully, the little iron-framed bed with the white spread across the mattress would be sufficient.

When Abigail looked at him, Grant saw nothing but gratitude in her gaze. "Thank you for everything."

Grant wished he could enjoy some quiet time with her, a moment of normalcy. But he knew that wasn't the case. There were details that needed to be attended to.

"I'm going to need to call your dad now," he reminded her.

She nodded. "Good luck."

Why did her words sound ominous?

Probably because they were.

EVEN THOUGH GRANT'S phone wasn't on speaker, Abigail still heard her father's voice coming through the cell phone.

She and Grant had gone back into the living room. While Abigail sat on the leather sofa, Grant paced in front of her, phone to his ear.

"What do you mean my house exploded?" her father practically shouted.

"It appears that the man who abducted your daughter also set a bomb at your house," Grant explained. "Abigail and I were just minutes away from being hurt ourselves."

Abigail waited to hear what her father would say, but she already knew he wasn't the type to show concern over her. He was all business all the time.

She didn't realize until recently just how much she resented that fact.

"I hired you to watch over her," her father grumbled. "Maybe I should rethink my offer."

Grant offered a sympathetic frown at Abigail. "I assure you that your daughter is doing fine. But we're going to need you to come back to Cape Corral so we can ask you some questions."

"I'm afraid I can't do that. Why don't you send one of your guys here to talk to me instead?"

Abigail blanched. Her father *would* think like that. Everything was always about him.

"We don't have the resources for that," Grant said. "Besides, it's your family and your property being targeted. I'm sure you want to figure out what's going on before there's any more destruction."

Her father didn't say anything for a moment. Abigail held her breath, halfway expecting him to scold Grant again before refusing to come.

Instead, he said, "Fine. My wife and I will be there Monday morning. But make it known that I'm not happy about this. This should be your job. My life shouldn't be turned upside down just because your police department is incompetent."

Grant's scowl darkened. "I assure you that we're not incompetent, sir."

"Could have fooled me. Ever since I've been on that island, you guys have acted like amateurs. This only goes to prove it."

Grant's chest expanded as he drew air into his lungs and then slowly released it. "It doesn't sound like I'm going to change your mind, so I won't waste my breath. But I'll see you on Monday."

Grant ended the call and shoved the phone back into his pocket. His gaze looked dark and stormy as he turned back to Abigail.

Her father had really upset him, hadn't he? Rightfully so.

"He can be difficult," Abigail finally said, hating the regret she felt. She couldn't control her father but she still felt responsible for his actions at times.

"Yes, he can be. I knew that before today."

The conversation continued to replay in her mind. How could Abigail's father not have asked about her? Her heart squeezed with grief.

Was that the kind of man her dad was? The kind who cared more about work and money than people?

She didn't have to ask herself that question.

Abigail knew that he was.

And she prayed she didn't turn out anything like him.

GRANT KNEW that Abigail had heard most of the conversation he'd had with her father. That couldn't have been easy. Heaviness still seemed to hang in the air between them, even though the call had ended several minutes ago.

"You've been through a lot," Grant said. "You probably want to turn in for the night."

"Actually, I could unwind a bit." Abigail pulled her legs beneath her, the oversized couch nearly drowning her.

"I could fix us some sandwiches. You're probably hungry."

"That sounds great. I can help."

Several minutes later, they sat down at the table with ham sandwiches and pretzels. They talked and ate and acted like nothing was wrong, even though everything was wrong.

When they finished, Grant insisted on cleaning up. As he put the last glass in the dishwasher, he turned and saw Abigail standing near the window, staring out at the dark ocean on the other side.

The view was one of his favorite things about his house—it was just one dune over from the Atlantic. Staring at the water always set his soul at ease.

He dried his hands on a dish towel before pacing toward Abigail. She continued staring outside even as he got closer.

She formed quite the picture as she stood there. Her hair was pulled up into a high bun again today. The style accentuated her long neck. Her arms were crossed in front of her, and her body language made her look pensive—as anyone would be in her situation.

Before Grant could second-guess himself, he put an arm around her waist and stared out the window with her. She leaned back into him as if they'd done this a thousand times before.

"Are you sure you're okay?" he asked softly in her ear.

"I don't know what I am anymore." As Abigail said the words, she turned and buried her head in his chest.

Grant pulled her closer, and she rested silently in his arms.

He wasn't complaining, nor would he stop her. He'd wait until she pulled away.

Finally, she stepped back just enough to look him in the eye. "What are we doing, Grant? We've been flirting for months."

His throat tightened as he stared at her. Something about her tone indicated she'd given a lot of thought to the question. That maybe her confusion even burdened her.

"You're fascinating, Abigail Ferguson. You're nothing like I thought you'd be."

"What do you mean?" She tilted her head as she stared up at him, her eyes probing his for answers.

"I mean, your family has a reputation. But I remember the first time I saw you, you were on the beach helping a tourist who'd cut his foot on a shell in the sand. That's when I knew you were different."

A small smile tugged at her lips as if his words had gotten through to her. "You want to know a secret?"

"If it's something you're sharing? Absolutely."

She tilted her head again, her features soft and open, almost as if she wanted to reveal her soul to him.

The thought delighted Grant more than it should.

"Seeing you when I'm running is the highlight of my day," she admitted.

A grin stretched across his lips. "I like that secret. I may or may not plan when I'm going to run based on when you're usually exercising."

"Then what are we doing?" She stiffened as if anticipating the conversation turning painful.

Grant wished he had a concrete answer for her. He'd thought about the two of them . . . a lot. The truth was, there was no simple solution.

"Abigail . . . do you realize what kind of storm would erupt with your family if we dated?"

"Absolutely." Abigail nodded, appearing unfazed.

"I don't want to put you in that position."

"Why don't you let me deal with them? I'm a big girl." Her voice sounded confident, sure.

"I'd love to do that. But there's one problem."

"What's that?"

Grant twisted his neck, wishing things were different. But he had to think clearly here instead of with his emotions. His heart wanted one thing, but his mind knew another.

"I've been hired to keep an eye on you. It wouldn't be very professional . . ." He stared at her lips, his throat going dry.

What was he going to say again?

All he could think about were her lips . . .

"It wouldn't be professional to do what?" Abigail asked, still staring up at him.

"It wouldn't be professional to . . ." Grant couldn't

take his eyes off her mouth. Couldn't stop imagining what her lips might feel like against his. Or what she might taste like.

He wanted to explore the soft skin of her neck. To feel her silky hair. To know if the fireworks between them existed as he imagined they did.

"Yes?" Abigail lifted her head.

"To do this . . ." Grant's lips met hers.

As they did, Abigail clutched his shirt, her body bending with his.

There was no hesitation—only a passion that had been pent up for entirely too long.

Soft skin?

Absolutely.

Silky hair?

Grant could run his fingers through it all day.

Fireworks?

Goodness gracious, yes.

All he wanted to do was to scoop her in his arms, carry her to the couch, and never stop kissing her.

But that would be a bad idea.

Instead, Grant forced himself to pull back. As he did, his heart still raced uncontrollably.

He never thought a kiss could shake him up like that. But it had.

And now he wanted more.

Later.

Maybe.

Abigail stared up at him, her gaze looking just as dazed as he felt. "Based on our earlier conversation, I'm going to assume we should probably pretend that didn't happen."

"There's no way I'm going to be able to forget." Grant started to lean forward again, not wanting this moment to end.

But as his phone rang, Grant knew any more talking—or kissing—would have to wait until later.

Maybe that was for the best.

CHAPTER TWENTY-ONE

AS GRANT TALKED on the phone, Abigail sank to the couch, trying to stop thinking about that kiss. Yet she couldn't. It replayed over and over in her mind.

Every wonderful moment of it.

She'd known Grant was a sweetheart. But that kiss ... it had been tender yet passionate.

It had been a long time since Abigail had felt a connection like that ... if ever.

How could she be falling in love with a man her family disdained? Did she want to set herself up for failure?

She had no idea. All she knew was that she practically felt like she was floating.

Grant put his phone back into his pocket and sat

down beside her, a pensive expression on his face. "Dawson has been cleared."

Nothing sobered Abigail more quickly than talking about this case and the peril surrounding her life. "You sound certain."

His jaw flexed. "The man has been in Mexico on a vacation for the past two days. It's been verified."

Abigail shook her head, still trying to make sense of that update. "Then what was he doing visiting Merle?"

"Apparently, Dawson and your father met at a restaurant down in Nags Head to catch up and maybe make amends," Grant said. "The waitress at the restaurant verifies she saw them together."

"Okay . . ." There was obviously more to this.

"After Dawson left, he stopped by the tackle shop. Merle used to take people on fishing charters sometimes, and, based on some evidence police found in Merle's shop, we believe Dawson is telling the truth when he says he was trying to book a trip for the spring."

Abigail felt her shoulders slump. "So that leaves us back at square one?"

Grant frowned apologetically. "I'm sorry, darling. I wish we had better news and that an end was in sight."

Any other time, she might melt at his affectionate nickname. But not now. "I suppose if Dawson was our guy, that would be too easy. Nothing about this situation is easy. In fact, to assume that the man behind these acts would brazenly show his face in public would probably be foolish. That man seems smarter than this."

"I agree."

Grant started to lean closer but stopped.

That was probably a good thing, Abigail realized. If he scooted too close, Abigail just might want to forget her problems by kissing him again.

While that would be a nice distraction, kissing would get them nowhere closer to finding any answers about the man tormenting Abigail.

Grant leaned back, though his gaze still studied hers. "Can I ask you some questions about your father?"

"Of course. What do you want to know?" She followed his lead and leaned into the soft cushions of the couch.

"Would you say your father makes most of his money from his financial investments or from real estate?"

She shrugged. "I wish I could tell you, but my

father doesn't really talk about finances. I just know that he loves making money."

"Why is he so obsessed with building here? Do you mind me asking that question?"

"No, I don't mind." But if Abigail didn't mind, then why did her neck feel so tight? She cleared her throat, determined to push through this. "I guess my father thinks this island is special. He thinks other people would pay a lot to experience a bit of that specialness."

"Doesn't he realize that a resort would take away from what makes this area special?"

The burden on her shoulders pressed harder, heavier. "His mind is set on doing this. You have to admit . . . this place is unique. People should get to enjoy some of it."

"Building here will ruin that very uniqueness," Grant stared at her. "Wait, are you saying you agree that this resort should be built?"

She opened her mouth before shutting it again. "I'm saying . . . I don't know. I can see both sides, I suppose."

Silence stretched between them a moment, and Abigail could feel the invisible barrier between them climbing higher and higher.

Finally, Abigail cleared her throat again. Maybe

she should turn the attention away from her own opinion. Besides, it would give Grant some time to keep processing his thoughts.

"It hasn't always been like this, you know. This wasn't my father's original plan. At first, he just wanted a place to get away. It's just been over the past couple of years that he's really tried to push this plan forward."

Grant's brown eyes remained on her, but not in a judgmental way. He had a way of being both affable and masculine at the same time. Balancing those two qualities required a special gifting. But Abigail did sense a new standoffishness about him.

"You don't know what changed his mind?" he asked.

Abigail shrugged, even though a thought swirled in her head. That thought involved a promise she'd made—a promise to stay quiet, to keep family matters private.

Grant leaned closer. "What is it? I feel like there's something you're not telling me."

Abigail glanced up, trying to figure out if she could trust Grant. She knew she could. Still, she hadn't told anybody this.

She drew in a deep breath before deciding to take the plunge. It would feel good to share the truth with someone else, and it might help explain to Grant a little about her family life.

"Truthfully, my mom was diagnosed with MS a couple of years ago," Abigail admitted. "That really changed our lives a lot."

"I'm sorry to hear that."

"She's okay . . . for now . . . but the doctors have told us that she'll go downhill eventually."

Grant's gaze softened. "That's got to be difficult."

"It is, but we're hanging in there. What else can you do?"

"Do you think that diagnosis has something to do with your father's decision to build here?"

That was a great question. "I can't pinpoint exactly what it is. Maybe my father likes to stay busy so he doesn't have to think about what's happening with my mother. I'm not really sure. But that's the other reason my father likes having me at home—so I can help my mom without everybody knowing what's going on."

"So nobody else knows?"

Abigail tucked her legs beneath her again. "Just me, my father, and my mother's doctor. I suppose Johnny knows too, but the only person Johnny ever thinks about is himself."

"I'm sorry to hear about what's going on with your mom. I really am, Abigail."

"Thank you. I appreciate that." She sucked in a breath before jumping into her next question. "Do you think something concerning my father's business might be the reason why this is happening?"

Abigail held her breath as she waited for Grant's answer.

GRANT DREW in a deep breath as Abigail's question echoed in his head. "That's a good question. Honestly, I don't want anything from this case to get between us and—"

"I know."

Abigail's hand covered his, startling him and making him entirely too aware of her presence.

"But I need to know the truth," she finished.

Grant shifted, unsure how his words would be received. He wanted to tell her the truth. But he also wanted to protect her from the truth. Was there a happy medium?

He wasn't sure.

He drew in a deep breath before saying, "From the encounters I've had with your dad . . . he seems like the type who'll do whatever is necessary to get what he wants."

Abigail frowned. "That's probably true."

"It's clear he's made a lot of people mad. The question is, *why* did he make them mad? Did he fire them unjustly? Did he cheat them out of something? Or is it even bigger than those potential issues?"

Abigail stared at him, her gaze searching his. "What do you mean?"

How did he even say this? "I mean, what other kinds of shady business deals has your father done? Have any of them caught up with him?"

Abigail rubbed the side of her face before wrapping her arms across her chest. Grant instantly missed her touch. Craved it, for that matter. But this wasn't the time to dwell on that.

"I want to deny any of that could be true," she said. "But I know I can't. He's my father, and I love him, but I don't always admire him."

The pieces still didn't fit together in Grant's mind. The woman he'd come to know didn't fit the facts in front of him.

"Then why do you keep working for your father?" he asked. "Is it because of your mom?"

Abigail shrugged. "I suppose that's most of it. She needs me. I don't feel like I can leave her at a time like this. From an early age, I was taught that loyalty was important."

"And your brother?"

"Johnny has always been on his own. I think my parents realized when he was young that there was no taming him. So that left everything on my shoulders."

He could only imagine how that made Abigail feel. "That's a lot of pressure on you."

"It is. But family's family. Even though my parents made mistakes, they're still my parents." She grabbed a pillow and pulled it across her chest.

"I know." Grant's voice came out as a soft whisper. "Come here."

The next instant, she was in his arms again.

He shouldn't tempt himself. He should hold this woman at a distance.

Yet he couldn't. And he didn't want to.

Instead, he was inexplicably drawn to the woman, despite their differences.

He wouldn't change that for the world.

"More than anything, I want to kiss you again," he murmured in her ear.

"But you can't . . ."

A frown tugged at his lips. "We shouldn't. Not now. Not until this case is resolved."

"I understand."

"But once you're not a part of this investigation . . . I definitely want to kiss you. As much as I can." He tucked her head beneath his chin.

"That's good," she whispered. "Because that's what I want too."

Warmth filled him. Could the two of them overcome the obstacles in front of them?

Grant hoped that answer was yes.

CHAPTER TWENTY-TWO

THEY THINK THEY'RE SMART. But they're not.

I'm always watching. I have the resources to do so. They'll never get ahead of me.

He knew Thomas Ferguson well enough to know what the man was thinking.

It wouldn't be enough just to kill the man's daughter. He needed to let Thomas know that he was serious. It would take time to build up to that level. His plan was like a business deal. The finale didn't happen all at once. There were kinks to be worked out first.

Was that how Thomas saw his daughter? Based on his experience, he'd say yes.

Thomas had never been the fatherly type. Sure, he liked to show off his kids, almost as if they were another trophy to display. But Thomas Ferguson never had moments of warmth with his offspring. No, he used his children as a means to get ahead.

And that's exactly what I'm doing now.

Sometimes, people didn't learn lessons the easy way. Thomas Ferguson fit that description. He'd been sending the man subtle hints as to what needed to happen in order to make things right.

But Thomas had ignored him. Called him stupid. Said that his opinion didn't matter.

But all of that would be changing.

Now, I have the upper hand.

He'd heard through the grapevine that Thomas was traveling back to this island on Monday.

He couldn't wait to see the man. Couldn't wait to see Thomas sweat.

Because before all of this was over, he *would* be sweating.

Abigail Ferguson was just a bystander. An innocent bystander. He regretted that. But sometimes a man had to do what he had to do.

He'd learned that from Thomas himself.

This was all about to be blown open.

And he was excited to be on the front lines, working as an operative to make it happen.

CHAPTER TWENTY-THREE

ABIGAIL AWOKE EARLY and decided to make some pancakes for Grant. She couldn't resist. Besides, cooking kept her mind off her troubles. Fixing breakfast was the least she could do after everything Grant had done for her.

Just as the batter of the last pancake bubbled on the griddle, Grant emerged from his room. Abigail's heart skipped a beat when she saw him.

The man looked so alluring with his messy hair and sleepy eyes. How had he said it earlier? Finer than a frog hair split four ways?

She smiled at the memory.

But the pleasant feelings lasted only a moment.

Everything that had happened slammed into her mind.

It would be a long time before she could forget about the danger that hunted her. As much as she would like to relish in this moment, to revel in her attraction to Grant, she knew that wouldn't be wise. So many obstacles stood in their way.

Grant paused, propping his hip against the kitchen counter and crossing his arms as he studied her. His voice sounded deep and throaty as he said, "Good morning."

"Good morning." Abigail hoped he didn't see the way her cheeks flushed. "I hope you don't mind me using your kitchen, but I was hungry. I thought you might be too."

"Pancakes sound great—they smell great also."

She flipped the last one before unplugging the griddle. "Great. Then let's eat."

They seated themselves at the table Abigail had already set. She'd also put out some coffee and orange juice.

The two of them sitting here felt a little too cozy, a little too normal. She probably shouldn't get used to it.

But while other little kids had dreamed about what it would be like to grow up to be rich, Abigail had dreamed about what it would be like to grow up and feel normal.

Her family's wealth had done nothing for her. It only had made her feel isolated and alone.

But she knew a lot of people—most people—wouldn't understand that.

After Grant prayed, they dug into their meal. Thankfully, the pancakes were tasty. Abigail wasn't the best cook, but she didn't let that stop her. Plus, the scent of maple syrup and whipped butter made her mind drift back to happier times—times when Lucia had cooked hearty breakfasts on Saturday mornings. It had been one of the highlights of Abigail's week.

Grant paused with his fork raised. "I have a question for you."

"What's that?" She had a feeling a loaded question was coming.

"How would you feel about going to church with me this morning?"

Abigail's throat tightened. "Church? Here? I've just been watching it online mostly. It seems easier."

Grant shrugged. "I know. But our community church is a really great place. I think you'll like it."

"You're not afraid of being seen with me?" Abigail watched his expression carefully, looking for any cracks, any signals about how he really felt.

Grant placed his elbows on the table and leaned

toward her. "Nothing about being seen with you scares me, Abigail."

Her cheeks warmed again. "Okay, so maybe being seen with me doesn't scare you, but you have to know there could be consequences."

"I thought about that. And I'm okay with any results of my actions."

"Even if it affects your job?" She continued to watch him and noticed that he squirmed just a touch.

He sighed and leaned back. "Honestly, that's one obstacle I still need to figure out. I don't want to lose the confidence of the people. But I do feel certain that if people here on the island gave you a chance, they would see what I see."

"You really think that?" Abigail had her doubts. Emotions were so high here on the island at times. Someone had even egged their house not long ago, just to let her family know they weren't welcome here.

"I do."

"Well, that's awfully sweet of you." She pushed some pancake around her plate.

Grant tilted his head. "So what do you say? When this is all over..."

"When this is all over, I'm willing to take the risk

if you are."

A grin stretched across his face. "That makes me a very happy man."

She leaned closer, wishing she could kiss him now. "That's what I want to hear . . . for a long time."

He reached forward and brushed a finger across her cheek. His touch caused tingles to shoot down her spine and back up again.

When he lowered his hand, Abigail instantly missed the connection.

"We have just enough time to eat and get ready before we go to church," he said. "We should probably stay focused."

"Probably."

But when Abigail saw the affection in his gaze, she knew today would be a better day. With Grant by her side, how could it not be?

GRANT FELT a surprising burst of pleasure at the thought of Abigail going to church with him. Yes, it would officially be the first time that the two of them would be seen out in public together. But it wasn't like they were being seen as a couple.

Or was it?

Because that's what Grant's heart desired. He wanted to show everyone that he and Abigail were an item.

But he also wanted everyone to understand that they couldn't judge a book by its cover. Just because Abigail's last name was Ferguson didn't mean she was a bad person.

After they finished eating, they cleaned up, got ready, and walked to the front door.

Abigail wore one of Emmy's old dresses, a navy-blue number with a flared skirt with little flowers on it. It didn't look like Abigail's usual designer clothes. But she still looked like a million bucks.

Grant twirled her around in a circle. "I declare, you look simply beautiful."

She always did. She'd look gorgeous even wearing a feed sack.

Her cheeks heated before she said, "You look nice too."

"Well, thank you, my dear." He ran a hand down the front of his white button-down shirt. "Are you ready for this?"

"As ready as I'll ever be." Abigail looped her arm through his as they walked toward the front door.

Grant prayed for the best. He knew that the people in town were good people. But even good people sometimes had misunderstandings or misconceptions that affected the way they acted. He hoped this wouldn't be one of those times—especially not at church.

After grabbing his keys from the table, he opened the door.

As he did, Grant stopped in his tracks.

His breath caught.

Another threat had been left for Abigail.

As he looked at the object on the ground, he saw a rag, as well as a bottle of something. Chloroform? That's what it appeared.

Beneath the bottle was another note.

It'll happen when you're least expecting it.

Grant glanced up at Abigail and saw her face had gone pale again.

This was yet another reminder that things were far from over.

CHAPTER TWENTY-FOUR

ABIGAIL TRIED to focus on the church service in the quaint little building with its arched roof and stained-glass windows. The scent inside reminded her of her grandmother's house—lemon furniture polish, old papers, and well-used carpet.

She'd gone to a large church in New York. Since she'd come here to Cape Corral, she'd watched services online most Sundays. She hadn't thought she'd be welcome with the island's only congregation. But she missed the in-person fellowship, and being here felt refreshing almost in an old-fashioned way.

As Abigail held the hymnal with Grant, her thoughts went back to the note that had been left on his porch and the silent threat behind it. Was she even safe here? The man had proven he knew no boundaries when it came to threatening her.

Church was known as a sanctuary, a place of safety. But was there anywhere Abigail would really be safe?

She couldn't let fear cripple her. She had to keep moving forward, had to show this guy she was stronger than whatever he threw at her.

All of that seemed easier when Grant was at her side.

They stood beside each other in church now, the congregation singing an old hymn, one she hadn't heard in years. "It Is Well with My Soul."

Something about the old song brought her a rush of comfort.

Her nanny used to sing it to herself as she'd cleaned.

Lucia had been one of the few people who'd actually cared about Abigail growing up, one of the few adults who'd taken time to listen to Abigail's dreams. Abigail treasured those times far more than any expensive gifts her parents had given her.

When Lucia quit, Abigail had felt heartbroken at the loss. None of her other nannies had lasted more than a few months. Maybe it had something to do with Johnny. He'd been a real handful, even as a child. He was still a handful today.

As they sat for the sermon, Grant leaned closer. "You doing okay?"

"I am. Thank you."

Grant slipped his arm around the back of the wooden pew, his hand brushing her shoulder. A rush of comfort filled her.

Could everything really be well with her soul? In the middle of the storm, could Abigail cling to the peace that passed all understanding?

She closed her eyes and lifted a silent prayer. *Lord, thank You for the blessings You've already blessed me with. Thank you for bringing Grant into my life. But, please, help me now. I need Your protection. Desperately. I'm afraid it's not only my life that depends on it.*

AS THE SERVICE ENDED, Grant stayed close to Abigail. So far, the outing had gone well. His friends had gone above and beyond to welcome Abigail. Several others had sent her polite smiles and nods.

He honestly hadn't been sure how things were going to play out this morning.

So far, so good.

Maybe there *was* hope for the two of them.

Grant led Abigail toward the exit, hoping he might talk her into a crab cake sandwich at Mrs. Minnie's place. A moment of normalcy would be nice—for both of them. Maybe Abigail would slowly get used to being around locals.

"I can't believe you would bring her here," someone in the distance said.

Grant's back muscles tightened.

He tugged Abigail closer as he turned and saw Florrie Mason standing near the door, a scowl on her wrinkled face.

Grant lifted a quick prayer for patience. The woman was known for being outspoken and opinionated—as well as difficult. "Now, Ms. Florrie. Have you met Abigail before?"

The woman's eyes narrowed even more as she pointed her cane at Abigail and shook her head. "I don't need to. She's a Ferguson. Have you forgotten what her family has done to this island?"

"Church is a place for everyone, no matter their background, their family, their past," Grant said. "It's a place where we come just as we are. Isn't that what Pastor Daniels talked about today?"

The woman still didn't look convinced. "She's not welcome here."

"We should go," Abigail murmured as she clung to his arm.

"Ms. Florrie . . . I mean no disrespect, but you know that's not true." Grant tried to keep the irritation from his voice, but it felt nearly impossible.

"You're going to need to choose your side—them or us!" Ms. Florrie leveled her gaze with Grant, challenge in her eyes.

"Ms. Florrie!" Pastor Brian appeared behind them, seeming to sense what they'd been talking about. He took her elbow and began to lead her away. "God loves all His children. He loved Jews and Gentiles. He loves locals and newcomers here on the island. You taught our kindergarten Sunday school class for years. You remember the song 'Jesus Loves the Little Children'? It talks about everyone being precious in His sight."

He led her down the steps, offering an apologetic glance at Abigail.

When they disappeared from earshot, Grant turned to Abigail. "I'm sorry about that."

She used a trembling hand to push a hair behind her ear. "It's okay. I should have expected it."

"No, you shouldn't have. Church should be a safe place for everyone. Yet we all come with our own flaws, I suppose."

She nodded slowly, almost resolutely. "My family has stirred up a lot of trouble on the island. I can't blame people for not liking me."

"They just need a little more time."

The two of them walked outside together, the sunlight feeling pleasantly warm amidst the forty-degree day. Levi and his wife, Dani, joined them, and the four of them chatted for several minutes.

Then Levi's faced turned serious, and he lowered his voice. "I wanted to let you know that we sent off a print on the bottle of chloroform."

"Maybe we'll get a hit."

Levi turned to Abigail. "This guy is going to mess up sometime, and, when he does, we're going to catch him."

"I hope you do," Abigail nearly whispered.

But laced within her words were doubts—most likely, about more than one thing.

CHAPTER TWENTY-FIVE

LEVI INVITED Grant and Abigail over to his place for lunch. Dani had fixed a seafood casserole, and several other people from the island had come, including Dash, his fiancé, Lizzie, and her son, Preston; Dillon and his wife, Gracie; and Emmy and Colby.

Abigail had been hesitant to say yes to the invitation. But now that she and Grant were here, she felt as if she'd been a part of the group for a long time. Everyone was friendly and didn't seem to give her last name a second thought.

Despite that, Ms. Florrie's words continued to run through her head. *She's not welcome here.*

Abigail feared everybody on the island thought as that woman did. It didn't matter how many times

Grant tried to reassure her, the fear still remained, nagging at the back of her mind. Abigail might live here, but she'd never be a true part of the community. She'd never be accepted.

Once they'd finished eating lunch and had tried some of the island's famous twelve-layer cake, Grant put his hand on Abigail's back. He didn't seem one bit ashamed to be with her.

Though the thought brought her comfort, she also had to weigh the risks she was bringing to Grant.

"We should probably get going," he murmured softly in her ear.

Abigail nodded, torn between regret for having to leave and relief to have some time alone to think.

Everyone waved goodbye or hugged her, and, for a moment, Abigail felt a strange sense of home.

What would it be like to permanently be part of this group? The idea intrigued her and stirred up a longing she didn't know she had. Though she valued her independence, the connectivity of Grant's friends captured her imagination—maybe even her hopes.

Just as the sun started to sink in the sky, they climbed into Grant's truck and started down the road back to Grant's place.

"So what did you think of the gang?" Grant asked.

"Your friends are great. I really appreciate them inviting us over."

"It wasn't that bad, was it?" He seemed to read the hesitation in her voice. "I mean, it was better than running barefoot through a field of wild roses, right?"

Abigail resisted a smile as she shook her head. "No, honestly, they were great. I can't say a bad thing about anybody at the house."

His smile sank. "I want to apologize again for what Ms. Florrie said at church. She was out of line."

Abigail waved a hand in the air, not wanting him to beat himself up over it. "You have no control over other people. Don't worry about it."

"Words can hurt, even the toughest of us."

"I'm not going to deny that."

"Listen, can I show you something?" Grant asked.

"Of course. What?"

He grinned. "You'll see."

They continued down the road—onto the land her father owned. As Grant pulled up to the top of one of the dunes, he put his truck in Park and stared out ahead.

Abigail followed his gaze and saw a harem of horses grazing there. There were probably eleven horses all together.

The scene looked so . . . peaceful.

She sat up straight. "Is that a foal?"

Grant nodded. "That's our newest one. She was born in the fall."

"She's beautiful."

"Isn't she?" Grant continued to stare ahead. "This is where your father wants to build his resort."

Her smile disappeared. "I know."

"It's also a place where these horses love to come. It's wide open. The trees on the west end of the island protect them from the elements. There are several ponds they drink from and plenty of acorns and persimmons to eat."

"In other words, it's perfect for them."

"It really is."

She glanced at Grant. "I get why you don't want the resort here. I really do. You want to protect these horses."

"They've been here for two hundred years. It seems a shame to ever develop this place. It will only result in putting these creatures in danger."

Abigail let his words linger in her mind. After a

few minutes of silence, Grant started the truck again and pulled away.

They'd have to pass Abigail's old house on their way. Part of her dreaded seeing the charred remains.

As they pulled closer to her house, something caught Abigail's gaze.

Someone was walking near the charred remains of her home.

She drew in a breath.

She knew exactly who that was.

The question was: what was he doing here?

GRANT BRISTLED as he saw the figure walking around near the rubble.

Was that . . . ?

He started to tell Abigail to stay where she was. Before he could, she opened the truck door and charged toward the figure in the distance.

Grant hurried after her.

He reached her just as she paused in front of her brother, Johnny Ferguson.

The man looked like an overgrown spoiled rich kid, and he didn't seem to mind that fact. His blond hair was stylishly messy, his clothes casual but expensive, and his grin cocky.

He looked like he'd just gotten back from a trip to the beach in his khaki shorts, T-shirt, and leather sandals. Even though it was January, his skin was still tan. Even his sunglasses screamed summertime affluence.

"What are you doing back here?" Abigail demanded, her hands fisted at her sides. "I thought you weren't returning from the Caribbean for another week."

Johnny shrugged and pushed his glasses to the top of his head. "What can I say? I got bored so I decided to come back early." His gaze flickered to Grant, and his eyes darkened. "What's he doing here?"

Abigail glanced back at Grant before raising her chin. "He's with me."

Johnny's eyebrows shot upward, and a humored look danced through his gaze. "Is that right?"

"That's not what I want to talk about right now," Abigail said. "When did you get back?"

"Late last night." Irritation crept into Johnny's voice. "What happened here? I was so tired when I got here yesterday that I barely had time to think about it. Instead, I just made myself at home at

Uncle Brian's place. I decided to come check things out when I woke up this morning . . . or, should I say, afternoon?"

"You didn't hear what happened?" Surprise— and a healthy dose of doubt—rushed through Abigail's voice.

"Obviously, I didn't or I wouldn't be asking."

Grant wedged himself in front of Abigail, not liking her brother's tone. "Someone set a bomb in your house, and it exploded yesterday."

Johnny's eyes widened. "What? Man, that stinks."

"That would be the understatement of the year." Grant tried to keep the sarcasm out of his voice but couldn't.

Johnny didn't seem to hear him. "Do you know who did this?"

"That's what we're trying to figure out," Grant said. "You don't have any ideas, do you?"

"No, why would I have any ideas?" Johnny sounded aghast at the suggestion. He turned from Grant and studied his sister's face for a moment. "What happened to you? It looks like you got into a fight or something."

Abigail shook her head, her features still pinched and her voice containing a hint of shock.

"You really have no idea what's happened over the past few days, do you?"

"Apparently not." The haughty look remained in Johnny's eyes, almost as if the two of them were inconveniencing him with this conversation.

"We should all have a talk," Grant said.

Johnny nodded toward a house in the distance. "Why don't we use Uncle Brian's place? It looks like that's where I'll be staying for a while."

Going inside sounded like a good idea. They were too exposed out here.

"Yes, let's do that," Grant said.

Grant walked across the sand with Abigail to another house equally as big as the Fergusons'. Abigail asked Johnny some mundane questions about his trip, and Johnny talked about everything as if he didn't have a care in the world.

Grant shouldn't be surprised. Johnny liked to think about himself. Grant had endured enough unpleasant encounters with the man to know that.

After they climbed the front steps, Johnny typed a code into the keypad and pushed the door open.

But as Grant glanced inside, he stiffened. A savory scent floated through the air, making it clear someone had been here very recently.

"No one's staying here?" Grant confirmed.

Johnny shook his head, the first hint of fear washing through his gaze. "No, no one should be."

Could the person behind these crimes be camping out here? This place would give him a bird's eye view of Thomas Ferguson's house.

Grant withdrew his gun and stepped forward. "Johnny, stay with your sister. I'll be back."

CHAPTER TWENTY-SIX

"DID the whole island go crazy in the time since I left?" Johnny muttered as he lingered beside Abigail, confusion rippling in his voice.

She tried not to scowl at her brother, though his statement was typical Johnny. "A lot's happened, to say the least."

His eyebrows flickered up in his stereotypical carefree, arrogant manner. "I'd say so."

Abigail's lungs felt tight as she remained near the front door and let her gaze roam her uncle's place. Someone had definitely been here cooking. It smelled like vegetable soup, if she had to guess. She knew that none of her other relatives were in town.

As her gaze went to the kitchen table, she saw the papers strewn there. She knew her uncle well enough to know that he wouldn't have left a mess before he left, especially when considering it was for an extended period of time.

Had someone been in here just moments before they'd arrived? Had this person heard them coming and fled?

Abigail shuddered.

She only hoped, if that was the case, that Grant was able to catch this guy. Her gut told her that would be too easy and that it probably wasn't going to happen, though.

"Dad didn't come?" Even Johnny sounded surprised about her father's decision to stay in New York amidst everything that had happened.

Abigail tried not to frown. "He said he's coming tomorrow."

"You'd figure he'd be right here if his house burned down." Even Johnny was scoffing at their father's actions—and that said a lot.

"Yes, you would figure that." Abigail clenched her jaw. She didn't want to badmouth her father. But she'd be lying if she said she wasn't disappointed in him.

Johnny turned toward her, some of his arrogance fading. "Do they know who left that bomb?"

"I don't think so. The police are still investigating."

"Good to know." As her brother paused, he looked her up and down as if seeing her for the first time. "New dress?"

Abigail rolled her eyes. "Is this really the time to question my fashion choices?"

That was so like her brother. He cared about all things superficial.

"It just looks different from your normal clothing. Calm down, Scabby Abby." He smirked.

That was her brother's favorite nickname, given to her when she'd regularly fallen and scraped up her knees as a child.

Yet with every new snippet of conversation, calming down seemed to be harder and harder—especially when her brother was so infuriating.

Abigail's gaze shot to the back of the house. Where was Grant? Was he okay? Had he found any other evidence?

The questions raced through her mind like horses at the Derby.

Finally, she heard footsteps from the other end of the house. Abigail knew there were two exterior doors on that side of the home. Grant must have gone out one of them.

But when a figure stepped into sight, it wasn't Grant.

"LOOK WHO I FOUND." Grant kept a firm grip on the intruder's arm as he shoved him into the room.

As he did, Grant spotted Abigail standing near the door with wide, surprised eyes.

He couldn't blame her.

In fact, he understood her shock.

Grant released him and crossed his arms, his muscles rigid and ready to act.

"Dawson?" Abigail asked, just above a whisper. "What are you doing here? I thought you were in Mexico."

Dawson scowled, daring Grant to touch him again as he brushed off his expensive linen shirt. "I came back early."

"My guess is you didn't go out of town at all." Grant narrowed his eyes at Dawson. "Why don't you tell us what you're doing here?"

Grant pointed to the couch and waited until Dawson sat. Then he stood over the man, just daring him to lie again.

If this man was responsible for inflicting pain on

Abigail then he needed to go to jail, and the sooner, the better. Grant wasn't a violent man, but, when he remembered the bruises on Abigail, a fury like he'd rarely felt rose up in him.

"I can explain." Dawson's words tumbled into each other as panic filled his gaze. "It's not what it looks like."

Fire ignited in Abigail's eyes. "First, you were seen talking to a man who was later murdered. Then I was taken to that very man's cabin and tortured. I'd say you have a lot of explaining to do."

"Tortured?" Johnny gaped beside her. "I definitely missed a lot."

Abigail cast him a dirty look—a well-deserved dirty look.

"Go ahead and explain," Grant growled, turning his attention back to Dawson.

"Your father . . ." Dawson's nostrils flared. "He had me sell off my share of the business before he made some new investments. He did it on purpose. He didn't want me to have any of the profits. Those investments made him millions."

"So now you're trying to ruin him?" Grant asked.

Dawson raised his hands in the air again. "I didn't say I was trying to ruin him. But I *was* trying to go behind him and buy up more land before he could, to somehow distract him before he began building his little resort."

Grant glared down at him. "Nothing has been approved to be built."

Dawson practically snorted. "That's what you think. But Thomas has a way of getting what he wants. You should check the bank accounts of some of the people on the county council. They're about to make a ruling that this resort is going to be allowed to be built. You can mark my words on that."

Grant felt more tension thread his muscles. "So you're saying you came here to Cape Corral to stop that?"

Dawson ran a hand through his thick, light brown hair. "I wasn't sure if I could stop the development or not, but I figured it was worth trying to pay those same people off."

"I need a name," Grant rumbled. "*Who* were you trying to pay off?"

"I can't—"

"You're going to want to tell me." Grant stepped closer and glared at the man.

"Okay, fine, fine. Someone named Anna Blair," Dawson rushed. "She's the weakest link out of everyone on the council. She's in debt, and she could use the money. Plus, she's an outsider. She's never really loved this island like some people do."

"And you thought that in order to pay Thomas Ferguson back for making you lose money that you'd also torture his daughter and blow up his house?" Grant needed to make sure he was following this man's logic.

Dawson's eyes widened. "What? No! I would never do that. Are you crazy?"

"Then explain why you *really* were talking to Merle," Grant continued to push. This was no time to play Mr. Nice Guy. People's lives depended on finding answers.

"Because Merle's cousin is also on the county council," Dawson rushed. "I was hoping to get through to him so he would get through to her."

"So the whole spiel about you booking a trip in the spring was just baloney?" Grant shouldn't be surprised.

"I really did try to book a trip for the spring," Dawson insisted. "I figured it would be my way of saying thank you. That trip costs thousands of dollars so it's great for his business."

Grant shook his head, not liking where any of this was going. He wasn't sure he believed any of it either. The man obviously wasn't opposed to lying when it protected his best interests.

"What are you doing in this house?" Grant continued.

"Thomas used to let me stay here sometimes. I remembered the code to get in. I figured there'd be no harm, no foul in staying."

"But there's no car outside."

"My helicopter brought me in, and I had somebody drive me down to the house. Whenever I need a ride, I just call Stan, and he takes me wherever I want to go. You can check with him."

Grant would definitely be doing that. "When did you really get into town?"

"I didn't arrive in Cape Corral until this morning," Dawson said. "I'll do whatever's necessary to prove it."

CHAPTER TWENTY-SEVEN

LEVI CAME to get Dawson and take him to the station for more questioning. As he did that, Abigail sat on the couch at her uncle's place and filled Johnny in on all that had happened.

Even though her brother had never been compassionate, so to speak, he'd listened and had the decency not to scoff as Abigail recounted her story.

As she finished, Johnny shook his head and leaned back in the high-end armchair across from her. "I can't believe all this happened. I'm sorry, sis. I really am."

"We all are." An edge of protectiveness crept into Grant's voice as he stepped into the conversation.

He'd been lingering in the background, almost as if waiting to act if Johnny stepped out of line.

Johnny leaned forward, resting his elbows on his thighs. "Do you really think Dawson was behind this? I never really liked the guy, but I can't see him doing something like this."

"When we looked into him earlier, the resort in Mexico where he was staying verified he was there," Grant said. "It turns out that one of his colleagues checked in under his name. The question is: did Dawson arrange that to cover his guilt or is it just a coincidence?"

"This is all a nightmare." Abigail rubbed her temples.

As she did, Grant rested his hand on her back and gently rubbed it.

Johnny watched them from his chair across from them, his eyebrows flickering up again. "You two? I never saw that one coming."

Abigail closed her eyes. "I really don't want to get into it with you now, Johnny."

"Does Dad know?"

"I think she said she didn't want to talk about it now," Grant said.

Johnny shrugged and raised his hands up as if surrendering. "I was just asking questions. No judgment. You can't drop this on me and expect no reaction."

Abigail didn't know about that. But she wasn't in the mood to argue either.

Johnny glanced around his uncle's place. "So, can I still stay here tonight?"

Grant narrowed his eyes. "No, this is now a secondary crime scene. We're going to need to go through this place and look for any evidence."

"So where *can* I stay?"

"There *is* an inn in town," Abigail suggested.

"That old place?" Johnny said it as if the residence was a dump, even though it clearly wasn't.

"Yes, that old place," Grant said.

Johnny frowned. "I think I'll see if I can remember the codes to any other houses first."

GRANT AND ABIGAIL climbed back into his truck as Johnny set out to find a place to stay. He had a cell phone and would call them if he needed to. He didn't seem overly concerned about his safety.

"I need to go back to the station for a little while." Grant started his engine.

"I expected that. It's fine."

Grant glanced at Abigail and saw the weariness in her gaze. He missed their times of meeting on the beach when she'd seemed invigorated after a long run. He missed hearing her laugh. Seeing the light in her eyes.

But he knew those things would return with time.

"You look exhausted," he said.

"Exhausted is the new refreshed." She flashed a tired grin. "At least, in my world."

"You wear it well, all things considered."

"Thank you . . . I guess."

He reached toward her and skimmed the side of her face with his knuckles. As he pulled his hand away, he grasped her fingers and pressed his lips into them. "Is there anything I can do for you?"

"Just keep doing sweet things like kissing the top of my hand, and I'll be a happy girl."

A soft smile tugged at his lips. "I think I can handle that."

She leaned her head back—more like it fell back into the seat. There was obviously a lot on her mind. "Do you think Dawson is responsible for everything that's happened?"

Grant instantly sobered when he heard the heaviness in her voice. "I wish I could give you an answer to that question. He seems like the most likely person to be behind this. But . . ."

"I can feel it in my gut, Grant."

"Feel what?" He stared at her, wondering where she was going with this.

"Something else bad is going to happen. This guy isn't going to deescalate. He's going to keep getting worse. When is he going to stop? What's it going to take?"

Grant said nothing. He didn't want to think about the likely outcome of her questions. She couldn't handle the harsh reality of it.

"Maybe he's waiting for my father to come so he can hurt us all," Abigail continued. "I really don't know, and I don't want to find out."

"I'm hoping we'll find answers before any of that happens."

"I hope that also."

Grant glanced in his rearview mirror and saw Johnny walking down the road to another one of the houses.

Grant didn't know if it was just him or not. But Johnny hadn't seemed entirely surprised by what had happened in his absence. Grant wanted to think it was because the man was careless.

But what if it was because he was involved?

Grant didn't dare voice that question out loud. Instead, he kept it tucked away in the back of his mind. He'd keep an eye on Abigail's brother, just in case.

He didn't know what possible motive Johnny might have. But when money was involved, there were always more than enough reasons.

CHAPTER TWENTY-EIGHT

ALL NIGHT, Abigail had dreaded seeing her father when the sun rose. She'd hardly been able to sleep.

When her dad got back into town, everything was going to change. She felt certain of it. It was better if she put some distance between her and Grant now before she got too attached. That was one of the reasons she'd turned in early last night instead of spending time with him. It would be easier this way—at least, it would in the long run.

As she finished drying her hair, she mentally rehashed everything that had happened yesterday. Dawson, as far as she knew, was still being held by the police as they verified his alibis. None of the other uncovered evidence had turned up anything.

Abigail wasn't sure if she felt safer or like danger was still on her heels.

Just before she went to meet Grant, her phone rang. It was her father.

"Abigail, I have some bad news," he started.

More bad news? What now? "What's going on?"

"I won't make it back until tonight," he said. "I need to wrap up this deal. Then I'll catch a plane and be right there. Can you tell Officer Matthews the update?"

She lowered herself onto the edge of her bed, a slight pounding beginning at her temples. "He's . . . he's expecting you this morning. It's important that he ask you some questions."

"I know, but these things happen. It's out of my control."

Abigail doubted that. Her father usually did whatever he wanted.

What he was really saying was that returning to Cape Corral wasn't important to him—that Abigail wasn't important.

"Your mother is having an episode, as well."

Abigail's stomach tightened at the mention of her mom. "Is she okay?"

"It's getting harder and harder to hide that something has changed with her. You'll see when we get there. Try to be strong for her."

Be strong for her? Of course, Abigail would do that. But when would her father see the pain Abigail had gone through? When would he care?

She didn't want to be selfish, but if being attacked didn't get her father's attention, what would?

After she ended the call, she stepped out into the hallway and found Grant putting away dishes in the kitchen.

As always, the sight of him took her breath away. Today, he wore a blue flannel shirt and well-fitting jeans with his cowboy boots. He could have stepped right out of her teenage fantasies and into her life.

"Good morning," he muttered, turning toward her.

She flashed a smile before breaking the news to him.

"I just got off the phone with my father. He won't be getting here until later today. He had something come up." She didn't bother to hide the disappointment in her voice.

"I see," Grant said. "Maybe that will work out in our favor."

That was *not* the reaction she'd expected. "How so?"

"It turns out that someone with the Forestry Division needs to take a trip up to Virginia. I thought it might be good for you to get away from this place for a little while."

"What's the trip for?"

"One of our mares was injured, and we need to take her to the recovery farm."

Abigail nodded. "Do you think it's safe for me to leave?"

"Either way, I won't let you out of my sight." He offered one of his rakish grins that seemed to melt her heart every time.

She just had one more question. "How can you even get a horse off the island right now? On a . . . boat?"

"We've actually been approved to use the temporary bridge that's been erected. Normally, it's just for construction vehicles, but the Department of Transportation is making an exception for us."

"Aren't you special?"

"Not me. It's the horse." Grant grinned.

"I see. Well, I think that sounds . . . fascinating."

Grant nodded. "Great. Do you think you can be ready to leave within the hour?"

"I'm ready to go now."

Grant's face sobered, and Abigail braced herself for a change in conversation—for bad news.

"There's one other thing I want to tell you," he started. "And it's only because I want to be honest with you and not keep you in the dark about things."

"What is it?" She nearly held her breath as she anticipated what he would say.

"That fingerprint on the bottle of chloroform," he started. "As soon as Levi put it into the system, he got a hit."

"Whose was it?" Her heart pounded in her ears as she waited to hear.

Grant frowned before saying, "Your brother's."

GRANT WATCHED ABIGAIL'S face as she processed that news. Her expression went from shock to denial then back to shock.

"My brother?" she repeated.

Grant had been dreading telling her this news. "I'm sorry."

Johnny had been in the system for a disorderly conduct arrest a few years ago.

"You think my brother is the one behind this?

That my brother could have beat me like he did? I would have known if it was him. I would have recognized something about him." Defiance hardened her voice as she shook her head.

"I don't have all the answers. But you have to admit that Johnny has motive."

"What do you think his motive could be?" She stared at him, an incredulous look in her gaze.

"You work for your father. I'm going to guess that you stand to gain more in the long run than your brother, who lives off his trust fund and parties. Your dad is intelligent enough to see that."

Abigail's gaze made it clear that she still didn't buy it. "So why would hurting me help Johnny ultimately get more money?"

"If you're out of the picture, then everything will go to your brother."

She leaned back and shook her head, still in denial. "I can't see it. Besides, I stand behind my earlier statement. I would have recognized Johnny's voice, even if he tried to disguise it."

"I'm not saying that your brother did this." Grant kept his voice even, trying not to stir up any more hard emotions. "I'm just saying that his print was found on the chloroform."

A new thought flickered in her gaze. "Did you bring Johnny in for questioning?"

"Levi did."

"And what did he say when Levi talked to him?"

Grant drew in a deep breath, hating the strain this was putting on her. But he had no choice except to move forward. "He admitted he saw a bottle of some sort at the house where he was staying. He said he picked it up to look at it, but then put it back down. Since it wasn't his house, he didn't think much about seeing the strange liquid. He said your uncle is always trying unusual medical alternatives to help him look younger."

Abigail pressed her lips together as if in deep thought. "If his story is true, then the person behind this could have planted that near Johnny. They could have hoped that he would pick it up and that later it would implicate him. Maybe the person behind this knew all along that this would happen."

Grant shrugged. "It's a possibility."

She stared at him. "But you don't think that's the case?"

"I'm just trying to follow the evidence. But, in the meantime, I think it would be good if you got away for a little while."

"Can I talk to him?"

"He's going to be interrogated by the guys at the station for most of the day today. But maybe when you get back."

Abigail nodded stiffly. "I see. Okay then."

Grant stared at her another moment, trying to ascertain her emotional state. She looked shaken but strong. Considering everything that had happened, she was handling this remarkably well.

"You ready to get going?" he asked. "We can grab some breakfast once we get off the island."

"Let's go."

Grant prayed that Abigail would have strength throughout this ordeal.

Because this wasn't getting any easier.

CHAPTER TWENTY-NINE

ABIGAIL'S MIND rushed as she and Grant traveled down the road, pulling the horse trailer behind them. Could Johnny really be behind all this? She knew that her brother was selfish. Everybody knew that. Johnny might even delight in that fact.

But would he go as far as to try to hurt Abigail for some kind of possible gain for himself? She didn't want to believe that. But she didn't want to be naïve either.

Did she really believe Johnny had found that bottle randomly and picked it up? That he set it back down only for the actual bad guy to grab it with Johnny's fingerprint on it?

The story seemed farfetched. But maybe it

wasn't. Maybe Abigail should give him the benefit of the doubt.

Or maybe she'd been giving Johnny the benefit of the doubt for entirely too long.

She wished she knew the answers, but she didn't. Hopefully, Levi and the gang would be able to figure out something through questioning him.

In the meantime, maybe it was best that Abigail was getting off this island for a few hours. Maybe the trip would somehow help her clear her head and see things more lucidly.

Grant was quiet beside her, giving her time alone with her thoughts. Abigail appreciated that. There was so much she appreciated about the man.

She only wished that the big pieces of their lives fit together better. At their core, the two of them were compatible. But she couldn't shed her background or her family or her career.

Could she?

She wished the answers were easy, but they weren't.

"I'm sorry that your father won't be coming until later," Grant finally said.

"I'm not surprised. That's how he's always been."

"With your mother and father both being so busy, who took care of you when you were little?"

"I had various nannies, but there was one that I had for about five years. At times, she felt like a mother to me. Lucia was nothing like my family. In fact, she's the one who told me about Jesus. She used to sing hymns to herself as she worked. *And* she would give me hugs. Nobody in my family is a hugger. But after Lucia used to hold me and rub my back as I fell asleep, I wondered how I could have lived without hugs for so long."

"It sounds like she was a real blessing to your life. Whatever happened to her?"

"She quit. I guess she couldn't handle working for the family. My mom said she called my brother and me spoiled brats. I never saw her again."

"You have no idea where she went?"

"I assumed she probably went to live with her oldest son—he was grown. I've often thought about trying to find her, but I never have. I'm not sure she'll want to see me."

"Maybe one day."

She nodded. "Maybe one day."

Silence fell for a moment before Grant finally said, "Can I ask you a question?"

"Of course."

"What is it that you want from your father?"

She thought about it for a moment. "I guess I just

wish he'd accept me for who I am and not who he wants me to be."

"What if that never happens?"

She looked at Grant, feeling startled at his question. "What do you mean?"

"I mean, what if you never reach that goal? It's something you can't control. What will you do then?"

Abigail thought about it before shrugging. "I don't know. I guess I'll move on."

"Will you be okay?"

"I'll have no other choice."

Grant remained quiet a moment before saying, "I can understand where you're coming from. For a long time, I wished I had a mom and dad who loved and accepted me. But I finally realized that I had to be okay with who I was without any parental approval. It was tough. I think we all want to make our parents happy. But, in the end you surround yourself with people who accept you for who you are."

She offered a grateful smile. "I'm sorry that you understand the struggle."

"We both have different backgrounds, for sure. But it is nice to have people who can relate to you."

A moment later, they turned off the main road

and onto a long dirt road just over the border in Virginia. Trees surrounded them for probably a half mile until the land cleared and several buildings came into view—an old farmhouse, a barn, and what Abigail assumed were some stables in the back, surrounded by a black fence.

"Is this it?" she asked.

"This is it. Triple J Ranch. I can't wait for you to meet the horses."

For the first time all morning, Abigail's heart lifted. "That sounds really nice. I can't wait either."

GRANT COULDN'T HELP but smile as he watched Abigail with the horses. She seemed to really love them and even told Grant about some horses her family had owned while she was growing up. Her father had eventually sold them, but she said she'd enjoyed riding when she was younger.

"So you bring the horses here when they're injured," she clarified. "And, once they're better, you bring them back to the island so they can be with their herd?"

He rubbed the side of Buttercup's face. The horse snorted and rubbed her face into his hand.

As the scent of hay and horses rose around him, Grant couldn't help but feel at home. Sunlight peeked in through slats in the walls of the barn, reminding them that the sun still shone, despite the storm in their lives. A few stray birds chirped on the beams above them.

Grant remembered Abigail's question about returning the horses. "I wish that was the case, but it's not. Once a horse has been around people and other domesticated horses, then the horse can never return to the wild."

"That seems cruel." She stepped closer to Buttercup, as if trying to offer her some comfort.

"Unfortunately, that's just the way it is. I know it seems harsh, but our horses thrive here. As you can see, they have a lot of land to run and they're very well taken care of."

She frowned at Buttercup again. "It just seems like they'd miss their families."

"They're surprisingly resilient. Just like people."

Abigail cut a sharp glance at him, almost as if she was wondering if he was sending her some subtle wisdom.

Grant wasn't consciously doing that. But he *did* feel like people were more resilient than they often got credit for. People had the capabilities to make tough decisions and to get through heartbreaking experiences. That was a beautiful part about life—the ability to bounce back.

"So I know what happens when a wild horse has to be domesticated," Abigail said. "But has a domesticated horse ever been released in the wild?"

Grant's eyebrows shot up as if the question surprised him. "There's only one case that I know of that happening. There was a man on the island who had a horse of his own. During a storm, his mare got out, and he wasn't able to locate her for a long time."

"What happened?"

"We thought the horse had died out there. But, about a year after that storm the mare was spotted on the island. She'd actually joined one of the harems."

"Wow, she just jumped right in, didn't she?"

"I guess you could say that. Obviously, this isn't ideal or what we want for the horses. But sometimes, I suppose that's out of our control. In this case, it worked out. Wanderlust flourished and did great. We didn't see any signs of disease on her."

"But don't you think that while the horses are domesticated, they lose some of their instincts?"

"There is a learning curve, but they do what they have to do to survive."

As Abigail nodded, Grant wondered exactly what was going through her head.

If he was lucky, she might open up to him later. But the two of them just seemed to keep taking two steps forward and one step back. In the end, he wasn't sure where they would end up.

CHAPTER THIRTY

ABIGAIL COULDN'T STOP THINKING about what Grant had said. As he wrapped up things at the Triple J Recovery Farm, the conversation replayed in her mind.

She could understand a wild horse being made into a domesticated one. But a domesticated horse being given the freedom to go wild?

Now *that* was a concept that fascinated her.

Probably because she related more to the domesticated horses than the wild ones.

She'd always been taken care of. She never wanted for anything. She'd never been without.

Overall, her life was easy, at least in terms of her needs being met. Abigail never received affection or loyalty from her family. But, that aside, she'd grown up with the proverbial silver spoon in her mouth.

What would she do if she was able to roam free one day? If she made her own way? Could she be resilient and survive, as Grant said the horses did? Could she pave her own way? Fend for herself?

She didn't know, but the idea intrigued her.

She rubbed Buttercup's head one more time before turning toward the door.

"You ready to head back?" Grant asked.

She nodded. "Yes. Let's get going."

Grant put his hand on her lower back, as he often did. And just as it happened every time, Abigail felt sparks shooting through her skin, her blood, even her bones.

No man had ever had this effect on her.

It seemed a shame to walk away from this kind of romance.

Then she remembered that her father was coming to the island later. Instantly, Abigail sobered.

She had some decisions to make.

GRANT COULD SENSE that Abigail had a lot on her mind. He wasn't sure exactly what it all was. Was it the fact that her brother could be guilty?

He didn't know.

But he couldn't stop thinking about what Abigail had told him either. He couldn't imagine what it would've been like to grow up without any hugs. It almost defined the phrase poor little rich girl.

It was a wonder she'd turned out as well as she did. Despite her upbringing, she was still warm, kind, and personable.

But she was also very much sheltered. Even though Abigail had told him that she'd worked on her own in New York, he still had to wonder how many of her needs were met by her father. Had he provided housing for her? Given her an allowance? Did she have a trust fund?

Grant would guess that the answers to those questions were yes.

What would it be like if Abigail was out in the real world? If she had to fend for herself?

Certainly, she could get a job doing something. She had two degrees from Princeton University, for goodness sake. Those would get her somewhere.

And crisis management? That definitely seemed like a career she could find somewhere.

On Cape Corral?

Grant didn't know. Still, so many things were

done virtually nowadays. It could be a possibility, right?

As they cruised down the road, he glanced into his sideview mirror. The same dark sedan with tinted windows had been behind him for the past twenty minutes.

Coincidence?

He couldn't say for sure. But he wasn't going to take any chances either.

Grant switched into the other lane to see what the other vehicle would do. The driver didn't switch immediately, but, several minutes later, the other driver also followed suit.

If he didn't know better, Grant would think he was being followed.

But what could the person behind them possibly want to accomplish by following Grant and Abigail right now?

Clearly, this man's goal was to torture both Abigail and her family. He'd made it clear that there was more coming, that there was *worse* coming.

But what would following them right now prove?

Grant didn't know, and he didn't want to find out. Mostly, he just wanted to keep Abigail safe.

"What are you looking at?" Abigail asked.

"Nothing." Grant tried to play it off.

"That car has been following us."

So Abigail *had* noticed. He shouldn't be surprised.

"It has been." Denying the fact would get them nowhere.

"Do you think the driver is the person behind these events?" Her voice trailed slightly as she said the words.

"It's a possibility."

She rubbed her throat, suddenly looking a little paler. "What are we going to do?"

"Once we reach the bridge, we'll be okay. Nobody else can cross it except us and construction workers."

"But how far away are we?"

"We've still got at least thirty minutes."

She frowned. "A lot can happen in thirty minutes."

Yes, a lot *could* happen.

Just seconds after she said the words, Grant felt his truck lurch.

That other driver had rammed his trailer.

His hands tightened on the steering wheel.

Just what was this guy up to? And how far was he going to take it?

CHAPTER THIRTY-ONE

ABIGAIL CLOSED her eyes as dread filled her. This was just one more way that man would try to torture her, wasn't it?

It didn't matter. All Abigail cared about was that she and Grant could be in danger right now. If that man hit them again, the trailer behind them could jackknife. They could get into an accident.

They weren't the only ones in danger—anyone around them could be as well.

"Hold on." Grant pressed down on the accelerator, and they sped down the road, faster than before.

She glanced into her sideview mirror. The car remained on their tail.

The next instant, she felt another nudge.

The car had hit them again. What was Grant

going to do? How are they going to get out of the situation?

Looking ahead, Abigail saw a line of stopped traffic.

They had to slow down.

Otherwise, they were going to hit those cars in front of them.

She glanced at Grant and saw his jaw tighten. He was feeling the pressure of the situation also.

He glanced into the mirror again before tapping the brakes.

Abigail braced herself, unsure of what would happen. What if the car slammed into them? If that was the case, then she doubted that the car would be able to take off. The other vehicle would probably be totaled.

What could the man possibly hope to prove by ending everything like that?

She glanced in the side mirror again, waiting to see what the driver would do next.

If only she could see through those windows. But they were tinted. She couldn't get a glimpse of who was inside. Not only that, but the car was so close that she couldn't even make out the license plate.

If the man behind them now was the person who'd committed the crimes against her, there was one positive. If Johnny was being held right now at the police station, then he obviously wasn't the one driving this vehicle. Her brother would be cleared.

The remaining suspects she might be able to handle, but she couldn't bring herself to consider that somebody blood-related might be doing this to her.

"He's going to hit us again, isn't he?" Abigail gripped the arm rest as trepidation flooded her.

"I don't know. It's anybody's guess right now."

Abigail closed her eyes again and waited to feel the impact of the crash.

GRANT HAD no choice but to stop. He couldn't risk putting other people in danger. Not only that, but there was nowhere to pull off on the side of the road —just a grassy median beside him. If he pulled over too quickly, he feared that his trailer would flip.

This guy was out of his mind.

As his truck came to a stop behind another vehicle, Grant glanced in his mirror again.

The car veered off the side of the road, cutting over the median.

The good news was they hadn't been hit.

The bad news was that the driver was getting away.

Grant couldn't let that happen.

"Hold on," he told Abigail again.

Abigail gasped as he turned and pulled across the median. His truck and trailer bounced over the elevated strip of grass.

As he glanced down the road, he saw that other car zooming away. The good news was that Grant had memorized the license plate. He'd definitely be calling it in as soon as he could.

For now, he wanted to catch this guy. This was his chance to get some answers—as long as he didn't put Abigail in danger.

Finally, he made it across the raised median and merged into traffic going in the opposite direction.

As he glanced ahead, he frowned.

Where had the car gone? It had just been there.

Even though the driver had gotten a considerable distance ahead of them, there was no way he could have actually disappeared.

He must have turned down another road.

Grant pressed the accelerator harder, determined to catch up.

But the car still didn't appear.

As he reached the next street—the nearest one—

he made a split-second decision and swerved onto the road.

"Did he go this way?" Abigail asked.

"That's what we need to figure out." He kept a tight grip on the steering wheel, adrenaline pumping through his blood.

They'd only gone a mile down the road when a sprawling, waterfront neighborhood appeared.

Grant ground his teeth together.

There were too many places for a man to hide in an area like this.

Despite that, Grant wasn't going to give up yet.

He handed Abigail his phone. "I need you to call in the license plate for me."

He rattled off Levi's number before telling her what the plate had read. Abigail recited the information, and Levi promised to look into it.

As Grant scanned another street, the black sedan was nowhere to be seen.

Somehow, that man had managed to get away.

His scowl deepened.

This was far from being over.

CHAPTER THIRTY-TWO

HE WAS SMARTER than they were.

When would they begin to understand that? And why did he feel like he needed to prove it to them?

Either way, he was having fun with the task, so he couldn't complain.

He hadn't really intended on nudging that trailer. He had only intended on following them for as long as he could.

Of course, the fact that they'd been able to cross the temporary bridge had thrown him off—especially since he could not. Instead, he'd borrowed a boat. Then he used a car that he kept on the other side of the water at the harbor there, and he waited until he saw Grant's truck pass.

It had taken the two of them at least an hour

longer than it had taken him, but he finally saw them coming. He pulled out behind them, and they'd been none the wiser.

He had really wanted to follow them onto the horse ranch itself. He'd schemed up ideas of ways he could torture them there. What if he had managed to get the horses to trample them? Now wouldn't that have been fun?

He smiled at the thought of it.

But it would've required more planning than he had been able to do. He couldn't take the risk of them seeing his face.

Not yet. That would come soon enough. He wanted them to be surprised. But first he needed Thomas Ferguson to get into town.

Nudging that trailer had been spontaneous. But he'd taken enough trips up and down this highway to know there was nowhere for Grant and Abigail to pull off. They'd had no choice but to keep going.

But he knew not to take it too far. He couldn't ruin his own vehicle. Thankfully, he'd been able to get away when he did.

He'd turned down a side street and into a little neighborhood. Someone there had left their garage open, and he'd simply pulled inside and lowered the door.

The homeowners were in their backyard. He could hear them. But they had no idea he was here.

That was okay. If they discovered him, he had a cover story. He was going to feign a memory issue. Tell them about the PTSD he suffered because he was a military veteran.

They might be suspicious at first, but eventually they would understand and let him go.

He had no doubt about that.

Now he just had to wait until he was certain that Grant and Abigail were heading back.

It was a good thing that patience was his middle name.

Because there was no way he was getting caught today.

There was too much on the line for him to let that happen.

CHAPTER THIRTY-THREE

ABIGAIL STILL FELT DAZED as they arrived at the station in Cape Corral. The ride home had been mostly quiet after the incident on the highway. Perhaps she and Grant were both lost in their own thoughts over what had happened.

There was certainly a lot to think about.

Grant had explained that they needed to drop off the now-dented trailer. After they did that and Grant parked beside the station, he assisted Abigail out of the truck.

"I need to run to my office for a minute," Grant said. "You okay with that?"

"Of course." She'd figured there would be paperwork or follow-up after what had happened.

As soon as the two of them stepped inside,

someone stormed from the waiting area and confronted them.

Her father.

Abigail sucked in a breath when she saw his flared nostrils.

Maybe she'd expected to see compassion or gratitude that she was still alive. But she should have known better.

Her father looked angry. His skin was red, all the way to his thinning hair. His body looked wired, almost like he was ready to fight. Every motion appeared brisk.

He barely gave Abigail a glance. All his attention was focused on Grant.

"Are you trying to put my daughter in danger?" Her father stared up at Grant, who stood a good foot taller than he did. That didn't deter him. "Why would you take her off the island at a time like this?"

Grant readjusted his hat, still appearing calm and cool. "I assure you that I've been keeping an eye on her."

"If you were doing your job, she would be safe right now."

"Father—" Abigail started.

"This is why no one takes the people here seriously," her dad continued. "You think you guys can be an isolated community that does what it wants, that's above the rules governing the rest of this state. That's not how democracy works."

"Money doesn't always win." A hint of irritation crept into Grant's voice. "And you should never mistake importance with how much wealth you have."

Pressure mounted inside Abigail as she realized the conversation—and tension—was escalating.

"I'm glad you made it back, Father." Abigail's voice sliced through the pressure mounting in the room.

Her dad's shoulders seemed to soften a moment as he turned to her. "Good to see you, Abigail. I'm sorry about all you've been through—both with the man who abducted you and this unreliable police department."

"The police here have been nothing but good to me," she told him. "They've gone above and beyond to ensure my safety, and they don't deserve to be spoken to like this."

Her father's gaze darkened, and she expected him to argue. Instead, he frowned and his gaze flickered back to Grant's.

"What do we need to do?"

Grant nodded toward a doorway in the distance. "Why don't we go into my office?"

"THE MAN who abducted Abigail told her to make sure her father does what he needs to do. What does that mean?" Grant leaned back in his chair and watched Mr. Ferguson closely, looking for any sign of deceit.

He wished Abigail wasn't here for this conversation, but she'd insisted. When her father hadn't pushed back, Grant had given her the go-ahead.

She stood near the door now, listening to everything.

"I have no idea," the man said. "That's what you're supposed to figure out."

"Since this man is obviously associated in some way with you, then we're going to need you to be more forthcoming with some details."

"I already told you, I have no idea what he is talking about. I've made a lot of enemies in my life. Business isn't always pretty, and it's not a place where everyone is your best friend. Maybe you should look at some of the locals around here.

Maybe they're doing this to dissuade me from building that resort."

"I highly doubt that any locals would take things this far. And we will look into anyone necessary in order to see that justice is served. But, sir, you need to realize that your daughter's life is still in danger. This man is still escalating, and he's still promising that there will be consequences if he doesn't get his way. Anything that we can do to head him off before he strikes again would help ensure the safety of your loved ones."

Mr. Ferguson scowled. "You can ensure the safety of my loved ones by keeping guard over us. I've already given you my list of suspects. There's nobody else that I can add."

Grant leaned forward. "Certainly, there has to be somebody else who could be guilty."

"You said you already have someone in custody."

"That person is not guilty," Grant said. "The person behind this followed us today. He's still out there."

"Followed you?" Mr. Ferguson let out a degrading chuckle. "You mean the guy was that close to you and you couldn't even catch him?"

"Believe me, we tried." Grant's eyes narrowed. "It

was more complicated than it might seem on the surface."

"Of course, it was more complicated for simpletons like the people around here."

"Father . . ." Abigail's eyes widened in horror. "There's no need to call names here."

"I'm only speaking the truth. You know it too."

"I don't agree with your assessment. I need to make that known."

Her father's eyes flashed with anger as he looked at her. "Can I have a word with you? Alone?"

CHAPTER THIRTY-FOUR

GRANT LEFT the office to give Abigail and her father a moment alone. Dread filled Abigail's stomach as she anticipated what her father might have to say. Based on the stormy look in his eyes, it wouldn't be good.

"You seem to have developed a soft spot for these people," he started.

"What's not to like about them? They've taken me into their homes and protected me. They have been nothing but kind."

He pressed his lips together before saying, "You know that they are against everything we stand for."

"Everything we stand for? I certainly hope that there's more that defines us than your desire to build a resort here on the island."

Her father's expression remained stiff and unchanging. "You know that our family's future depends on this resort."

She stared at her father another moment. "What does that mean?"

"That means we need to make this happen. That's all you need to know."

Something about his words caught her off guard. "Are you having financial troubles?"

His gaze darkened. "I wouldn't say that. But you know your mother is not going to be getting any better—we've tried the alternative treatments, and they haven't worked. We need to make sure that she's taken care of."

His response didn't sit right with her. "I've always helped out with mom. You know that."

"If you start associating with these other people, I'm not sure what that means for your future..."

Abigail stared at her father, uncertain exactly what he was saying. She thought she knew, but certainly she was misunderstanding something. "Why can't I be a part of this family and be friends with the locals?"

"Because the two don't mix. We need to keep our distance if we're going to get what I want. It's just going to be easier that way." He said it so matter-of-factly, as if Abigail was too dense to understand.

She crossed her arms, feeling a surge of outrage —and offense. "I don't agree. I think your approach to this is all wrong."

Her father's eyes narrowed, almost as if he didn't respect her opinion. "Now that your mother and I are back, you can come home and stay with us."

"Our home burned down. Do I need to remind you of that?"

"We'll be staying at Vince's place," he said. "You can join us."

Vince was her dad's first cousin, and he worked in some way for her father's company.

Abigail raised her chin as she contemplated her options. "What if I don't want to?"

Finally, her father's expression broke. He stared at her with something close to shock in his gaze. "Are you saying that you would choose *them* above *us*?"

He said it as if locals were enemies or disease-ridden lepers unworthy to mingle with the upper class.

"I'm saying that I shouldn't have to choose at all." Abigail raised her chin even higher. You're being unreasonable."

"I'm going to bring in some new bodyguards for you. They'll be staying at the house, and they'll make sure that nothing happens to you."

"Grant's the only one I want."

Realization seemed to dawn in her father's eyes. "Is that right? You're falling for this guy?"

"So what if I am?" Abigail kept her voice firm and determined. She often capitulated to her father's demands—but that was getting old. Besides, she was a grown woman. Maybe coming to work for her father had been a terrible idea.

Then again, she might not have ever met Grant if she hadn't.

"He will never fit in with our family." Her father's words almost sounded like a warning.

She fisted her hands at her side. "You can't mean that."

"I'm dead serious, Abigail. There's no room in your life for him. It's going to be a choice between him and your family. So you need to think this over long and hard."

With those words, her father rose and stormed from the office.

Her father had just rejected her, she realized. While Abigail shouldn't be surprised, she couldn't stop the shock from rolling through her.

She'd hoped that, when it came down to it, that her father would be reasonable. That he would give Grant a chance. That he would consider her feelings.

But she should have known better.

What was she going to do?

GRANT WATCHED as Mr. Ferguson stormed away. When he stepped into the office, Abigail looked just as he thought she would.

Devastated.

He stepped inside and closed the door behind him. In three strides, he met her and pulled her into his arms.

"You had a rough talk, I assume."

"You could say that," Abigail said. "My father is just so unreasonable."

"I'm sorry." Grant knew there was nothing else that he could say. Nothing that would make this situation better.

Abigail let out a sigh, and she suddenly looked exhausted, like all this was taking a toll on her. "We're still no closer to finding any answers either, are we?"

He shook his head. "The license plate we ran came

from a stolen vehicle near the North Carolina/South Carolina border. I figured this guy was too smart to let us track him that way. Your father certainly wasn't very forthcoming with any information he might know."

"I suppose I shouldn't be surprised."

"I'm sorry you're going through this, Abigail. I really am."

"What do we do now?" She glanced up at him.

When he saw her wide eyes, his heart seemed to stutter for several beats. This woman was so beautiful in so many ways. Grant hated seeing her go through all this pain.

He'd done everything in his power to take it away from her, but so far that had led nowhere. The man who'd hurt her was still out there, and the man who should love her the most wasn't offering any help in finding him.

"We're going to keep doing everything within our power to find him," Grant insisted.

Abigail pulled back slightly and ran her hands over her face, as if trying to gain control of her emotions. She let out several deep breaths before her gaze met Grant's.

"I can't believe he's being so unreasonable." She frowned, her thoughts clearly still on her father. "I don't know what to do. My father pretty much told me that I have to choose between my family and this town."

"He actually said that?" Grant knew the man had a lot of nerve, but surprise—and shock—still filled him.

"Not in so many words, but yes. That's basically what he told me. The thing is, I can't turn my back on my mother when she needs me. Apparently, just in the week that they've been gone, she's taken a turn for the worse. If I'm not there to help her, then who will be? Certainly not my father. He'll busy himself with work."

"I'm surprised your father hasn't hired a nurse."

"Never show weakness. That's my father's motto. He's very private about things like this."

"I can only imagine what a hard spot you're in." Grant paused. "You really think your father would disown you over this?"

Abigail was quiet a moment before nodding her head. "I do. He got mad at his own father about ten years ago and didn't speak to him afterward—not even when he was on his deathbed. If there's anything my dad knows how to do, it's how to hold a grudge."

Grant frowned. "I guess you need to weigh the risks and rewards. Make a pro and con chart."

Abigail hardly seemed to hear him. "If my father really disowns me, I'll have no job and no family."

"I'm sure you can get another job." Grant rubbed her arm, desperate to offer her some kind of comfort. But he couldn't even begin to imagine what she was going through.

"Maybe . . . but not here in Cape Corral. This place isn't exactly big enough to employ a full-time crisis management public relations firm."

Grant frowned as he realized her words were true. "No, it's not."

Her wide eyes looked up at him, questions hovering there. "I don't know what to do, Grant. I don't want to choose."

He stepped closer and lowered his voice. "I'm sorry, Abigail. I can't make the decision for you. This is something you have to do on your own."

Even as Grant said the words, he certainly knew what he *hoped* Abigail would do.

But what if he was hoping for too much? Besides, he had his own set of issues to deal with when it came to his feelings for Abigail Ferguson.

It appeared that nothing about their relationship was simple.

CHAPTER THIRTY-FIVE

AS ABIGAIL LOOKED up at Grant, her heart filled with warmth. The fact that he hadn't pressured her to make one decision over another was just one more thing to love about him.

Love about him? No, they weren't there yet. But Abigail could feel something building between them.

Why couldn't her father see how special Grant was? Instead, he focused on the fact that Grant opposed building this new resort. As a law enforcement officer on this island, Grant had been working hard to stop it from happening.

Abigail could see both sides of this coin.

But when she looked inside herself to figure out what she thought was right, she knew this island would be better off without that resort her father desperately wanted.

Abigail cleared her throat. "There's one other thing he said that I thought I should mention."

"What's that?" Grant's full attention was on her.

Part of Abigail felt like she was betraying her father by saying this, but he'd left her with no choice. "I don't know what's going on with my father's financial situation, but he hinted that he needed this resort to be built to fulfill some type of monetary obligation or hole in his portfolio."

Grant squinted. "Do you know what that means?"

She shook her head. "As far as I know, our finances are in good shape. But he wouldn't tell me if they weren't, and I don't have access to his books."

Grant frowned, appearing deep in thought. "How is it possible that his finances are out of order?"

"Easy. When you're making big investments, you're taking big risks." Abigail shrugged. "If one thing falls through, that affects everything else as well. I'm not saying that's what happened. But maybe that would explain a little bit more why my father wants this resort to be built so much. Maybe it's more than him *wanting* it to be built. Maybe he *needs* for it to be built."

Grant crossed his arms, his expression stony with thought. "But still, even if this resort happened, it's still years away from opening. Once he gets all the permits and secures the financing, then he has to begin the building process and establish the correct infrastructure here on the island. It's not a get rich quick scheme."

"I understand that. Like I said, I don't know any details. Honestly, I never really wanted to know what goes on behind the scenes with my father and his business dealings. Maybe I should have taken more interest."

Grant's gaze softened. "You couldn't have known."

Abigail shook her head, still feeling a bit hollow inside at the mess around her. "No, I suppose I couldn't have."

As she looked up at Grant, she again marveled at the man before her. She could easily envision her future with him. The problem was that everything seemed to be working against them.

She was going to have to make some decisions soon and take a stand. Her life, any way she looked at it, would be changed.

She wasn't sure exactly what she thought about that. She was used to dealing with crises at work, but, in her real life, she craved peace and acceptance. She wished everyone would just get along and try to understand both sides of an argument.

"What are you thinking?" Grant squinted as he studied her face.

Abigail's eyes went to his lips. "You really want to know?"

He stepped closer. "I do."

She rested her hands on his solid chest. "Okay, then. I'm thinking about how much I really want to kiss you again."

He tugged her closer. "I guess your father did officially fire me, so maybe there's no more professional conflict."

"I kind of like the sound of that." Her gaze remained on his lips. Those full, luscious lips. She knew what his mouth felt like against hers, and she wanted to feel it again.

Before she could second-guess herself, she stood on her tiptoes and pressed her lips into his. Grant didn't resist. His arms wound more tightly around her until their bodies melded snug against each other.

Then their lips explored each other's. Pent-up passion that had been building seemed to explode between them.

When Abigail finally pulled away, she felt dazed from the exchange.

Her connection to this man . . . it was more than just skin deep. It almost felt like their souls were intertwined.

She'd never experienced a feeling like this before.

And Abigail was quite certain she would never experience it again . . . unless it was with Grant.

GRANT'S HEART thumped out of control after that kiss. It had taken his breath away, to say the least. He could see himself doing that for the rest of his life.

And that wasn't something he'd said many times before.

He pushed hair from Abigail's eyes, his other arm still wrapped around her waist as they stared at each other. As much as he'd simply like to enjoy the moment, he knew there were other things they needed to talk about.

"What would you like for me to do from here forward?" he asked Abigail. "You can stay at my place or you can go back with your family. It's your call."

She nibbled on her bottom lip for a moment before slowly nodding with decision. "What I *want* to do is to go back to your place and stay there with you. But what I *need* to do is go and check on my mom."

Grant would be lying if he said disappointment didn't fill him. He wanted Abigail to come back with him. He wanted to protect her. To keep her in his sights.

But the decision *was* her call. He didn't want to be responsible for any regret she felt one day.

"I understand," he said quietly.

"I just need to figure things out," Abigail rushed, as if afraid he'd misread her choice. "To do that, I will need a little time. Please, don't take this as a rejection—"

"I don't." Yet part of him did.

What Grant really wanted was for Abigail to walk away from her family and their manipulative ways. It wouldn't surprise him if Mr. Ferguson's whole spiel about her mom getting worse was just a part of his plan to control her.

But Abigail had to figure that out for herself.

"I need you to be safe." The words nearly caught in Grant's throat.

"My dad said he's hired a few bodyguards. It

won't be the same as you. But maybe this will be better. If you're not with me all the time, then maybe you'll have more time to figure out who this guy is."

Her words contained a trace of truth. But there was nothing more that Grant wanted than to be the one who watched over her. Forever.

"I understand." He grabbed his keys from his desk, trying to ignore the somberness surrounding him. "How about if I take you back to where your family is staying?"

As Abigail nodded, Grant saw the sorrow in her gaze. She didn't want this any more than he did.

But how were the two of them ever going to make this work with all the obstacles standing between them?

That had been the question from the start, and it appeared they were no closer to finding that answer.

CHAPTER THIRTY-SIX

REGRET STILL SWIRLED inside Abigail as she sat across from her mom at the kitchen table in her uncle's home. Her father was on a phone call in his office, and Johnny had decided to camp out at another one of the family's houses on the island so he could have some privacy.

Grant had brought her to the house, walked her inside to make sure that everything was safe, and then stepped back. Both her mom and dad had shot him dirty looks the entire time he was inside.

Abigail was fairly certain the only reason Grant had left was because the three bodyguards her father had called were already here. Apparently, her father had brought them with him when he came into town.

As Abigail drank a cup of tea, she observed her mother, looking for signs that she was doing worse, as her father said. But her mom seemed the same.

Abigail knew that diseases didn't always manifest themselves in physical ways. And she didn't want to question her father. But with everything going on, it was hard not to.

What she really wanted was for her father to give Grant a chance. She wanted her family to show a little concern for her. To be willing to help find the person who had done this to her.

But instead, her father remained the cold, heartless man he'd always been. How could her mother have ever fallen in love with him?

"I'm glad you're okay." Her mom lowered her teacup, and the porcelain rattled against the saucer as it came down. "Your father and I were both worried about you."

A smart remark played on the tip of Abigail's tongue, but she held it inside. "I'm glad you're here now. How are you feeling?"

She fanned herself with the magazine in her lap. "Your father is worried about me, but I'm fine. My doctor says the prognosis for my disease is good."

"I'm glad to hear that."

Her mom narrowed her eyes. "You're not looking

well. Your eyes . . . they look dull. I see the bruises on your face, even though you're trying to cover them up."

Abigail briefly considered opening up to her mom about everything that had happened and everything she was going through. Would her mom be able to give her dating advice? Wisdom about her future?

She doubted it.

She and her mother had never had that kind of relationship.

Instead, Abigail shrugged. "I'm just exhausted after everything that's happened."

Her mother frowned. "Maybe you should turn in for the night."

"You know what? That's a good idea." Abigail stood from the table and lifted her cup so she could put it in the sink. "I'll see you in the morning, and we can catch up more then."

With that, Abigail dropped off her cup and then slipped into one of the guest rooms. She nodded to the bodyguard standing outside her door as she did.

She didn't want this bodyguard. No, she wanted Grant.

But reality was setting in. She was going to have to choose between her family and Grant.

GRANT SAT in his truck outside Abigail's house. He knew there were three bodyguards inside, but he still wanted to keep an eye on Abigail himself. This was the best solution he could think of considering the circumstances.

The darkness outside made it almost impossible to see anything.

What was Abigail doing? All the lights inside the house appeared to be off. The time on his clock read two a.m. Most likely, everybody was sleeping.

He had to wonder what tomorrow would hold for them. Would he see Abigail? Would she decide to walk away from the life her family had given her and find a new life with Grant? Or were the comforts and security of money too much to say no to?

Grant thought he knew Abigail well enough to know the answer. But people had surprised him more than once.

People like Charlotte, who'd made every decision about her future based on money. She'd chosen that over happiness with Grant. Though he didn't resent the choice now, it had been a hard pill to swallow at the time.

Grant only wished he had more answers.

His phone buzzed, and he frowned as he glanced at the screen. Why was Levi calling?

He quickly answered. "What's going on?"

"Our horses got out from the stable."

Grant straightened. "What? How did that happen?"

"I have no idea. My guess is that someone did it on purpose. We're out searching the south end of the island. You're up north, right?"

"That's right." Grant had mentioned to Levi what he was doing.

"Are you able to drive around and see if you can spot any of them?"

"Of course." The last thing they wanted was for their domesticated horses to be roaming with these wild horses. It was best to keep them separate. Plus, there were all kinds of dangers out here.

As he ended the call, Grant glanced at the house one more time. He'd patrol this area but stay close. He didn't want anyone getting to Abigail.

But right now, he had to help find the horses before they got hurt.

CHAPTER THIRTY-SEVEN

ABIGAIL FELT that something was off as she drifted in and out of consciousness.

She tried to pull herself awake.

But it was no use.

Her dreams and reality collided.

What was happening? Why couldn't she pull herself from this deep state of unconsciousness?

Push through, Abigail. You can do it. Force yourself awake.

Yet she couldn't. Everything was hazy and black around her. Nothing made sense.

Drugged.

She'd been drugged?

But what sense would that make? Besides, a

bodyguard had been stationed outside her door. No one could have gotten past him, right?

But something was wrong. She had no doubt about that. As soon as she was able to pull her eyes open, she'd figure out what it was.

But, by then, would it be too late?

Even in her sleepy state, she felt the cry building in her throat, a cry that wanted to emerge.

She was moving.

She felt certain that she was no longer in her bed. There was too much jostling. Too much movement.

Had someone drugged her and was now carrying her to another location?

Despair bit deeper. That was her best guess.

She was powerless to do anything about it. She tried to cry out, but no sound would escape.

She was at the mercy of a man who very well might kill her.

GRANT CIRCLED the northern end of the island several times, and he'd managed to locate one of the horses. He'd assumed that they would all stay together, but they hadn't.

He had no choice but to get out of his truck and corral Sugar Loaf. He then called Levi to let him know what was happening.

Grant tied Sugar Loaf up to a post near one of the houses. He couldn't afford to ride the horse back to the station right now. He wanted to keep an eye on Abigail's place.

Still, finding the horse and trying to capture him had probably taken at least an hour.

While he'd been working, Grant kept his ears open for signs of anything suspicious around him.

He hadn't heard anything, but he still didn't feel confident.

He hurried back to Abigail's house and stared at the place. All the lights were still off as if nothing had changed.

Was there something different about the place?

He didn't know. He couldn't pinpoint anything in particular. Maybe he was just feeling paranoid since he had been gone for so long.

But what he really wanted was to be inside that house. He wanted to have his eyes on Abigail.

But he had to work with what he had right now.

Just then, the front door of the home opened, and someone ran outside.

Grant sat up straight.

It wasn't Mr. Ferguson.

Was that one of the bodyguards that had been hired? It was too dark to tell. But the man looked fit.

Grant drew his gun and climbed from his truck as the man ran down the stairs.

The tension between his shoulders threaded more tightly.

The man stopped in front of Grant and their eyes met. If Grant remembered correctly, this was Ethan with Starboard Security.

"What's going on?"

The man sucked in a deep breath, still looking out of sorts. "Some type of gas was released in the house. It knocked us all out cold. When we all came to, Abigail was gone."

Grant's heart thumped in his ears. He wished he'd heard the man incorrectly. But he knew he hadn't.

The man terrorizing Abigail had seized the opportunity and had grabbed her.

Now Grant needed to find him before he got too far away.

CHAPTER THIRTY-EIGHT

ABIGAIL FINALLY MANAGED to pull her eyes open. Even as she did, her head swirled.

Where was she?

Just as when she'd been abducted before, darkness stood guard around her. She could hardly make out anything.

Except she knew for certain she wasn't at the house where she'd fallen asleep.

This place . . . it was too frigid. It smelled old and musty, like time and bad memories had been suspended inside the walls for decades. The material beneath her felt ratty, like matted carpet.

She tugged at her arms. They were tied behind her. Her ankles were bound also.

She lay on the floor, a wall behind her.

What had happened?

She remembered going to sleep. She recalled that feeling of being jostled.

Somehow, she'd been drugged and taken to a new location.

How had that man gotten past her bodyguards?

Had they been drugged also? It was the only thing that made sense.

Panic began to rise in her, but she pushed it back down.

Focus on what's critical.

Every decision should be informed.

Never panic.

Abigail had told herself those things before. Now she needed to remember them again.

Because she had no doubt another nightmare was lurking just out of sight. Maybe she could get these ropes off. Maybe she could run, escape.

A shadow moved in front of her.

She sucked in a breath. Maybe the nightmare wasn't out of sight.

He was here.

It was him.

The man.

The one who'd caused so much pain.

What did he want now?

Please, Lord . . . help me.

BETWEEN THE MISSING horses and Abigail's abduction, it was all hands on deck. The volunteer firefighters and patrol officers had been called in to help. There was no time to waste.

As much as Grant wanted to go into the house and look for clues as to what had happened, finding Abigail took first priority. He had to keep looking around this island for her before the man who'd abducted her got too far away.

A set of tire tracks appeared in the sand, and Grant tried to follow them from beneath the house. How had this guy gotten a vehicle here? If he was as smart as he seemed, he could have borrowed one of the ones the Fergusons left here for the winter. That was Grant's best guess.

He pictured a dark SUV pulling up to the house with no lights on. It was so dark out here with only a sliver of the moon that the man would have blended right in with the night.

If Grant had to guess, the man had released some type of sleeping agent through the air vents of the house where the Fergusons were staying.

This man was smart. Grant had known that from the start.

He must have released those horses, knowing that doing so would distract law enforcement on the island. As soon as Grant had left, the man must have come here to enact his plan.

The man had been swift. He'd had all these details worked out probably from the start.

As Grant reached the ocean side of the dune, still following the tire tracks, he paused and frowned.

Tracks lined the wet sand up and down the coast. It would be virtually impossible to trace this one set among the many here from the vehicles that had been off-roading.

The man had probably known that also.

As Grant looked up and down the shore now, there wasn't a car in sight. This man could be anywhere at this point.

And that was something that was unacceptable to Grant.

He had to figure out another way to find Abigail.

There was no time to lose.

CHAPTER THIRTY-NINE

"WELL, WELL, WELL." The man paced closer toward her, his footsteps light against the carpeted floor. "Here we are again."

Abigail managed to sit up, despite her bindings. She scooted closer to the wall behind her, pressing herself into it. "Who are you?"

That was the main question on her mind. What was this man's identity? He'd been taunting her, teasing her, maybe even dropping clues. But she had no idea.

He paused in front of her and put his hands on his hips. He almost sounded amused as he said, "You still don't know?"

"I don't. Why don't you just tell me?"

"That would make this all not as fun," he taunted.

She tugged at the ropes on her wrists, wishing they weren't so tight. But they were. She didn't know how she would get her bonds off. "What do you want from me?"

"I want your father to pay."

Abigail shook her head, wishing his words made sense. Wishing she knew what sin her father had committed against this man. "I don't understand . . ."

"He took something precious from me. Now I'm going to take precious things from him." The taunting left his voice, replaced with vindication.

Her throat went a little drier. "Money is what my father really cares about. You want to take away something he cares about, take that." Abigail's voice quivered with the words.

"I plan on taking that also. Don't you worry. But I thought I'd start with you."

"What did my dad ever do to you?" This was obviously personal. Whatever had happened felt like an intentional attack on this man.

"You really don't know, do you?" Surprise saturated the man's voice.

Abigail shook her head. "I can only assume it

was a bad business deal. That's usually the path of destruction my father leaves behind him."

"Destruction is a good word. A very good word. That is what your father does. He only thinks about himself." The man backed away from her and stood, glancing around. "That's why I brought you here."

She scanned the area around her again, looking for a clue to her whereabouts. Her eyes had adjusted some to the darkness—enough that she could make out an old house. Dusty drapes hung from the windows. A mounted fish was on the wall. A kitchenette made up one corner.

But she still had no idea where exactly this house was located. "Where am I?"

"This is one of the houses your father bought. It's on the property your father wants to develop for his resort. I thought it would be poetic to come here. Besides, this place is an old shack. No one ever even looks twice at it."

So they were still on Cape Corral. That was good to know.

Most of the land her father had been buying up was close to the northern side of the island. A few of the original island homes were still in this area. But it was like the man said, most of them had been neglected for years before her father bought them.

The only people that usually came up this way were the Fergusons.

"I've been thinking about this for a long time," the man said. "A *long* time. And I am sorry that you had to get involved with this. I always thought that you were nice."

So Abigail knew him. She'd known him for a while, it sounded like.

He definitely wasn't her brother. But she'd known that.

The man was too thin to be Dawson.

Johnny and Dawson had been the two main suspects the police were talking to. If it wasn't one of them, then who could this man be?

The way the man talked, there was obviously some affiliation that Abigail should be putting together.

But what was it?

"It's not going to work for your father to find you and for you to look nice and pretty," the man's voice dipped, his underlying threat clear in his menacing tone. "He needs to know that I mean business."

"You tried that before, and it didn't work. I'm telling you that if you want to target my father then you should target his money."

"That's a fine argument that you're going with. But what fun would that be?"

As he raised his fist, Abigail braced herself for the pain she knew was coming.

"I'M tired of the games you've been playing," Grant told Thomas Ferguson as the two faced off inside the home where the Fergusons were staying. "I need the truth. Your daughter's life depends on it."

Mr. Ferguson's face fell with the first dose of humility Grant had ever seen on the man.

"I'm telling you the truth when I tell you I don't know what's going on." Emotion made the man's thin voice crack.

Grant still felt bristly as he stared at Mr. Ferguson. "My question is, what do you know that you're not saying?"

He ran a hand over his eyes. "I received a blackmail attempt about a month ago. I brushed it off."

Grant's spine straightened. "What did it say?"

"It was an email. Whoever wrote it basically said that I needed to hand over five hundred thousand dollars or there would be consequences."

"You didn't go to the police with that information?" He didn't bother to keep the surprise or disgust out of his voice.

Mr. Ferguson shrugged. "I thought he was bluffing. Plus, I figured the police wouldn't be able to do anything. I hired my own private detective to look into it, but he couldn't trace the sender."

His words made Grant's blood heat with irritation. "All those things would have been valuable to know from the start. It might have saved us time, and your daughter would not be in the hands of a madman right now."

Mr. Ferguson narrowed his eyes, his features pinched. "I didn't think it was important, okay? I don't want to see anything happen to Abigail either."

His regret seemed a little too late. "I need to see that email."

"Of course."

Mr. Ferguson scurried to the other side of the room before returning with his laptop. A few minutes later, he had the email on his screen.

"The sender's email address was simply gimme@yahoo.com," Mr. Ferguson said.

Grant had to push down his emotions—his anger—as he read the email. The best thing he could do was let his logic take charge. "Did this private investigator you hired try to trace the email address?"

"He did, but he had no luck."

"And there are no shady deals you haven't told me about that this might go back to?" Grant wouldn't put anything past the man at this point. He was only looking out for one person—himself.

"I meant it when I told you earlier that it might be someone here on the island who was trying to make my life miserable. But I really don't know other than that." Mr. Ferguson shrugged. "I don't know what you want me to say."

What Grant wanted was the truth. "Were there any other follow-up notes or threats after this one?"

"I got this email." Mr. Ferguson clicked on something else on his computer.

Grant peered over his shoulder and saw another message. This one said, *I'm still waiting.*

"A week after that, I got one final email," Mr. Ferguson continued, almost as if suppressing a sigh. "He said, 'This is your last chance.'"

"During those times you didn't happen to think your family might need extra protection or that maybe you should take other precautions?" Grant was amazed that a man so smart could be so ignorant—and selfish. It was all a convoluted rigmarole of an excuse if you asked Grant.

"No, I didn't." Mr. Ferguson looked away, as if unable to make eye contact.

"That could have been a very costly oversight—not in terms of your net worth, but in terms of the people you're supposed to take care of."

His eyes met Grant's again, and the first touch of sincerity rang through his voice. "What can I do?"

Grant locked his gaze on Mr. Ferguson's. "You can tell me all the secrets that have put your family in danger."

CHAPTER FORTY

ABIGAIL WAITED to feel the man's punches.

But the impact never came.

She held her breath, anticipating, dreading.

But there was nothing.

Finally, she plucked one eye open.

The man still stood in front of her, his fist raised.

Her body remained tense as she anticipated what would happen next.

Finally, he lowered his arm, his eyes narrowed. "I suppose there will be time for that later. Why have all of my fun over with right now?"

Relief flooded her—however momentary. "What are you going to do? Wait?"

"I have a better idea." He pulled something from his pocket.

A phone.

He tapped a few things on the screen. Abigail had the distinct feeling his camera was open or that he was videoing something.

"I want you to send a message to your father," he finally growled.

"What message is that?" She shuddered as she waited.

"Tell him that this is the last time he's going to see you alive unless he gets me that money."

"What money?" She almost didn't want to know the answer to that question.

"A half million dollars. It's the least your father can do after what he did to me and my family."

"You and your family? What does that mean?" Abigail knew there was a clue buried in his words, but she didn't know what.

The man said nothing, only stared at her with something close to pity in his gaze.

"What would you do if someone did this to your family? What if I was your daughter?"

The man's gaze narrowed. "Don't play mind games with me."

"I'm not playing mind games with you. I just have no idea what's going on here. No idea why you are targeting me. I may be Thomas Ferguson's daughter, but that doesn't mean each decision he makes is something I should pay for."

"If that's the case, then why are you working for him?" His voice turned to more of a growl.

She shrugged. "Family should be there for each other. My father needed help, and I was qualified."

"You should be careful whom you affiliate yourself with."

"I was born into this family, so I'm affiliated with them whether I want to be or not. If you let me talk to my father, I can make sure he gets you that money."

"He's had his chance. I told him a month ago that I wanted it."

Alarm raced through Abigail. A month ago? Her father had been sitting on that information this long? And he hadn't offered it when Grant had talked to him and tried to get any details that could help them put this guy behind bars?

A new rush of disgust rose in her. She was no longer proud to say that she was her father's daughter. It was increasingly clear where his priorities were.

Even if she got out of this situation, things would never return to normal. She knew that.

She would always love her father. It was ingrained in her.

But that did *not* mean she had to like him or that she had to go along with his decisions.

Not anymore.

When Abigail got out of this situation, she was going to make a fresh start for herself.

But first she had to concentrate on surviving.

GRANT MET Levi outside the house a few minutes later. So far, nobody had located Abigail. It wasn't the news Grant wanted to hear. He could hear the ticking bomb in his head.

They had to figure this out, and they had no time to stand here. They needed to get moving.

"There's something else I don't understand." Grant shifted. "This person managed to rig sleeping gas into the Ferguson's heating system. First of all, that's no small task. But secondly, where did this guy get sleeping gas?"

"I had those exact same thoughts," Levi said. "I had Ron Jarvis look into it. You know that he used to be military."

"Okay . . ." Grant couldn't wait to hear where Levi

was going with this. Ron Jarvis was the island's HVAC guy.

"Turns out, the canister left there was military grade."

Grant sucked in a breath. "So the person behind this is former military?"

"That would be my guess," Levi said. "Maybe it was someone disgruntled when they left the service. Or some type of bomb or explosive special weapons expert. Those would be the people who'd be able to get their hands on something like this."

"At least, that might narrow our suspects down." Grant shook his head. "But that doesn't fit with our theory that this has something to do with one of Thomas Ferguson's former business deals. As far as I know, none of his deals involved the military."

"I agree. But maybe it's something we should look into. It might help to explain how this guy has been so qualified to carry out everything he's done so far."

"I'll go talk to Mr. Ferguson again."

"We'll keep looking," Levi said. "The good news is I think that we narrowed Abigail's whereabouts to a twenty-minute driving radius of this house. That's about all the time this guy had to get away. We'll go door to door until we find her, if that is what we have to do."

"Thanks. That sounds good." Grant hoped—and prayed—that was enough.

"We're going to find her," Levi assured him, his voice quieting with compassion.

Grant appreciated his friend's understanding and determination. "Thanks. If I hear anything from Mr. Ferguson, I'll let you know."

But in his mind, that clock kept ticking and ticking and ticking.

CHAPTER FORTY-ONE

"FATHER, if you're watching this, right now I'm okay." Abigail stared into the lens on the man's phone. "But I won't be for long. You had your chance to make things right, but you haven't done it. Your decisions don't just affect you, but they affect your family. They affect the people around you. Affect the people you employ."

The man in front of her nodded, indicating Abigail should keep reading from the script that he held.

She felt like one of those people in the videos that terrorists made to send to the media.

She had always hated seeing them. Hated the desperation. The isolation.

But here she was, feeling like she had no choice but to comply right now.

"I need you to send that money to a bank account," she continued, her voice trembling. "The routing number will be sent to you. Don't try to trace it. You have three hours, and three hours is all. Not a moment more."

The man turned the phone to himself. "Wait for my email for further instructions. You've brought this upon yourself. You have to know that. If you'd ever thought of someone besides yourself for even one moment, you wouldn't be in this situation right now. But you make decisions without regard to anybody else. That's all going to come to an end. I need that money or the next time you see your daughter, it will be at her funeral. Don't test me."

Abigail shuddered again as the man tapped a few things on the screen and lowered his phone before looking back at her.

"Sent," he announced.

Acid rose in her throat, threatening to materialize. She had no doubt that the man would carry through with that threat. His voice didn't even waver with doubt. He'd clearly meant those words.

How much longer did she have? He'd said three hours. But could her dad even get that kind of money in that amount of time? The banks weren't open right now.

The only comfort she found was in the thought that she was still here in Cape Corral. Three hours was plenty of time to search this island.

Maybe Grant would find her.

Hope pressed into her, begging her to hold on and cling to it.

Dear Lord, please help me. Please let them find me. I want to make things right. I want to undo some of the wrongs my father has created.

And I want Grant to know just how much he means to me.

She only hoped she had a chance to do that, especially after everything they'd been through.

Things couldn't end this way ... could they?

GRANT'S STOMACH roiled as he and Thomas Ferguson watched the video of Abigail.

She looked so alone, so scared.

Yet a touch of defiance remained in her gaze.

Good. That defiance might keep her alive.

But three hours?

That wasn't much time to find her.

He called the update in to Levi, who said they were still searching. There weren't but so many places on this island where this guy could be hiding.

They were going to find him.

"There's something else I need to speak with you about," Grant told Mr. Ferguson.

He hadn't had time to ask the man his other questions yet. As soon as Grant had come inside, the video had shown up on Mr. Ferguson's phone.

"Go ahead."

"Who have you worked with who has ties to the military?" Grant watched the man's expression carefully, looking for any signs of deceit.

Mr. Ferguson blanched. "The military? I don't work with the military."

"You've never worked with a paramilitary organization or tried to do a deal with someone with that affiliation?"

"No, never."

"Then who do you know outside of work who's in the military?"

Mr. Ferguson stared into the distance for a minute before shaking his head. "I really can't say I know of anyone. I'm in the business world and those are the people I work with. I don't have anything to do with the military."

"Are you sure you haven't tried to do any back-room deals?" Grant wasn't letting him off the hook that easily.

"I promise, I haven't. Real estate is my thing. I haven't done anything illegal that would put our country or troops at risk. I promise." Mr. Ferguson raised his hand, as if pledging his honesty. "Now, if you don't mind, I need to transfer some money. It's going to take all of three hours to do so."

Grant stood, hating the fact that he was getting nowhere with this man.

"There is one person I can think of that we know," Mrs. Ferguson said from the corner.

Grant paused and glanced at the woman who'd been largely silent since all of this happened. She looked frailer than he remembered—or was that because he knew about her MS? It didn't matter right now.

"Who?" Grant's back muscles tightened as he waited for her response.

She exchanged a glance with her husband before diving in.

CHAPTER FORTY-TWO

ABIGAIL WATCHED the man as he paced around the small house. What was he thinking? Did she really want to know?

And did she really even have three hours?

That was the real question.

Maybe this man didn't intend on letting her out alive.

He glanced at his phone again as he paced.

"Did you get the money yet?" Abigail licked her lips, wishing she had some balm with her. Still, that was the least of her problems right now.

"Not yet. Let's hope your father comes through."

She said nothing. She wanted to assure this man that her father would do as the man had demanded.

Yet she couldn't do that. She had no idea what her father was thinking.

Instead, she pressed herself into the wall and waited.

She liked to imagine that Grant was close. That he had somehow discovered her location and that he'd be barging inside anytime now.

But she also needed to be smart. Maybe she could somehow come up with a plan to get out of here herself if it came down to it. However, she couldn't do anything with these ropes preventing her from moving.

"Do you remember when you lived down in Miami?" The man paced in front of her.

Her breath caught. How did the man know she'd lived in Miami?

"I do." Her voice trembled.

"You had that penthouse apartment with the great views of the ocean. I have to say, I kind of like the views here more. It's more natural, isn't it?"

"How do you know about that penthouse?" Abigail's voice continued to waver with confusion.

The man continued to pace, reminding her of a lawyer at trial. "Do you remember drawing that hopscotch board on the cement outside your house?"

"I do. I didn't even know what hopscotch was before that day."

"Then your dad came home and was so angry with you, even though it was just chalk that you used and it would have washed off."

Her cheeks heated at the memory. The man knew exactly what he was talking about. That was what had happened, detail for detail.

Who was with her that day? Who would have known about that? Or had she told someone that story? Stephen, her ex-fiancé, maybe?

"I always thought your father was wrong to do that." The man clucked his tongue to show disapproval.

"How do you know about that?" Abigail's question came out barely above a whisper.

She didn't know where this was going, but she didn't like it.

The man continued to pace. "I have my ways."

"Did you work for my father?"

"No, I didn't."

Abigail searched her memories of that day, tried to remember who exactly had been there when that ordeal had happened. The whole thing had totally been blown out of proportion. Someone would have thought that Abigail had stolen something or cheated on a test. Instead, she'd written in chalk on the cement outside the patio of her house.

Had Dawson been there that day? It seemed like he and her father were business partners at that point. It was a possibility.

Had Abigail had a friend over? She squeezed her eyes shut.

She didn't think so.

Lucia had taught her about hopscotch. Abigail had thought it was the most wonderful thing ever. She had said that she was going to go outside every day to play it.

Before her father had ruined her plans.

But that still didn't tell Abigail who this man was.

She knew she was getting closer to an answer, though. If only she could remember . . .

Look at every detail.

Abigail would guess this man was in his early thirties. He had some type of military background. He knew about the hopscotch incident, so he had some kind of affiliation with her or her family.

But once Abigail put all of that together, whose picture formed?

The answer was on the cusp of her consciousness.

"WHO IS JOSEPH JONES?" Grant stared at Mrs. Ferguson as she sat in an armchair in the corner working on a crossword puzzle. She'd been quietly listening to their conversation this whole time. But now it was her turn to answer some questions.

"He's the youngest son of our former live-in nanny, Lucia. Abigail just loved Lucia."

"That's right." Grant nodded slowly as details clicked in place. "Abigail mentioned her to me once."

"Lucia was wonderful." Mrs. Ferguson frowned and set her puzzle book on the table beside her.

"Wanda . . ." Mr. Ferguson looked at her, something close to a warning in his gaze.

"Our daughter's life is on the line." Mrs. Ferguson shook her head, her eyes wide with indignation and repugnance. "I'm not going to hold back, not if it might help Abigail be rescued."

"What happened with Lucia?" Grant's voice sliced through the tension. "Why did she leave after all those years?"

"I'm not proud of it." Mrs. Ferguson glanced at her hands in her lap. "What it really boiled down to was the fact that I was . . . I was jealous."

"Wanda . . ." Mr. Ferguson warned again.

"Why would you be jealous?" Grant was determined not to detour this conversation.

She glanced up, moisture in her gaze. "Truthfully, my daughter always liked Lucia more than she ever liked me. I've never been the motherly type. But Lucia was. Abigail's face absolutely lit up every time she saw the woman."

"So you fired her?"

Mrs. Ferguson glanced at her husband before pressing her lips together, as if there was something she didn't want to say.

"What is it?" Grant pushed.

"The truth was I couldn't just fire her," Wanda finally said. "Then I'd end up paying her unemployment. There were all kinds of nasty legal matters that I could have gotten tangled up in."

That sounded like some kind of excuse Mr. Ferguson would have fed her. He seemed like the paranoid type, especially when it came to his money.

"So what did you do?" Grant crossed his arms as he waited for the rest of the story.

Mrs. Ferguson glanced at her husband again, and the sorrow on her face deepened. "I planted a piece of my jewelry in her bag. Then we staged it to make it look like Lucia had stolen it. I told her I wouldn't press charges if she left without issue."

Disgust roiled in Grant's stomach. None of this should surprise him—yet it did. The depths of selfishness in this family were astounding.

"How did Lucia handle that news?" he asked.

Mrs. Ferguson at least had the decency to frown. "She cried—desperately. She said she loved Abigail as if she were her own daughter. That's when I knew I had done the right thing."

Based on the defiant look in the woman's eyes, she didn't regret the decision.

"But she left?" Grant clarified.

"She did," Wanda said. "Abigail was heartbroken."

Of course she was. The one person who'd shown Abigail any affection was sent away without explanation.

Indignation welled in him. "Where did Lucia go?"

"I don't know." Wanda shrugged, almost as if a moment of apathy had returned. "I never heard from her after that."

"What about her youngest son, this Joseph guy?"

She let out a long breath and looked away, as if

her mind was traveling back to a different time. "Lucia was fighting for custody of him. Her ex-husband had full-time guardianship, but she was working hard so Joseph could live with her. Joseph was probably . . . I don't know . . . four years older than Abigail. On occasion, he came over to play with her."

Grant tried to put all the pieces in place. "So when Lucia got fired, there's a chance that, without any financial means, she would have been denied custody of her son?"

Mrs. Ferguson nodded, at least having the decency to avert her gaze and look ashamed. "That's right."

Grant didn't have time to dwell on those poor choices now, not when Abigail's life was on the line. But a clearer picture of this family was forming—one he didn't like. It only made him want to protect Abigail more.

"Why do you think it might be Joseph who's behind this?" he asked.

"He was in the military," Mr. Ferguson said. "I'm nearly certain that he was a weapons specialist."

"How do you know that?" Grant clarified. "I didn't think you kept in touch with them."

"About a year ago, we ran into Joseph. Or should I say, he found us and confronted us. Told us about his life after his mom was fired." Mrs. Ferguson's voice broke. "And now he's getting the ultimate revenge, isn't he?"

CHAPTER FORTY-THREE

"I ALWAYS FELT sorry for you, you know." The man continued to stand in front of her, almost as if lording the fact that Abigail had no control and that he was above her.

Abigail swallowed hard, concentrating on her breathing and remaining calm. She breathed in and out. In and out. In and out.

Focusing on something other than her fear was good for her. Dwelling on what made her anxious would only make her more anxious.

She glanced up at her captor. "Why do you feel sorry for me?"

"My parents . . . they both loved me so much that they fought over who got to keep me. Your parents don't seem like either of them really care. It's almost like you're more of an accessory or a beautiful piece of jewelry."

Abigail's heart thumped several beats. She wanted to argue with the man's assessment, but she couldn't. He'd hit the nail on the head, so to speak.

Plus, he indicated that his parents had been divorced and that there'd been a custody battle. It was one more clue that she tried to piece with the others in her mind.

"My mom really loved you," the man said.

His mom?

Abigail sucked in a breath.

"Joseph," she nearly whispered. "Lucia's son."

A smirk stretched through his gaze. "It's about time you caught on. I tried to drop some clues for you."

"You used to play with me when your mom brought you over, usually on those weekends when she had custody."

"Do you know what a shame it was that she had to work full time to take care of somebody else's child, so much so that she couldn't even take care of me?" Bitterness tinged his voice.

Abigail's throat burned. "I can only imagine how difficult that was."

"I didn't resent you for it. Not for the longest

time. At least, not until your family fired my mother."

"Fired her? What are you talking about? She quit."

He let out a bitter chuckle. "Is that what they told you?"

"Yes, that's what they told me. Why do you think differently?" Abigail wasn't sure she wanted to know. She could sense the pressure rising in the room.

"Your mother didn't tell you how she hid jewelry in my mom's possessions and then accused her of stealing it?" His accusation was clear—as was his resentment.

Abigail gasped at his words. She wanted to refute them—but she couldn't. She wouldn't put it past her family to do something like that.

"No . . . I had no idea . . ."

"I thought that you might eventually one day look for her and let her know how much she meant to you. Maybe you'd even try to make things right. But you didn't." His voice hardened again.

"I thought about looking for her several times. But I hadn't heard from Lucia either. My parents told me I was being difficult and that's why Lucia left. They said she didn't ever want to see me again."

"And you believed them?"

Abigail shrugged. "I didn't have a reason not to."

Joseph began pacing in front of her, the motion almost frenzied. "She died a year ago. Cancer."

"I am so sorry to hear that. I really am. She was a great woman."

He paused and stared at her again, more accusation in his gaze. "Do you know what happened to her after your father fired her?"

Abigail shook her head, her gut telling her this was only going to get worse. "I have no idea."

"She couldn't find a new job. Any prospects of getting full-time custody of me went out the window. She finally began renting a room and working at a little drugstore. She barely made enough to make ends meet. Even when her knees hurt from arthritis, she had no choice but to be on her feet all day so she could earn a paycheck."

"I'm so sorry. I had no idea."

"Of course you didn't. Because you're a *Ferguson*." He said the family name as if it were a bad word. "Fergusons only think about themselves."

"I don't want to be like that. I try not to be like my family." As Joseph looked away, Abigail tugged at the ropes around her wrists. He was going to blow up at any minute. She couldn't just sit here.

"But can you help that?" He practically spat out

the words. "What if selfishness is just in your blood?"

"We always have a choice on how to live our lives, no matter how we're raised or whose blood we have going through our veins. Our character is determined by the choices that we make." Abigail believed those words. She really did. She hadn't perfected them, but she was trying.

"That's poetic. I like it. But what have your choices said about you? You did come here to work for your father." He leered over her, challenge in his gaze.

They'd been over this. But that probably didn't matter, did it? Joseph had obviously had a lot of time to let his resentment build.

"I don't want to be like my father," Abigail told him. "In fact, I want to build a very different life than my father."

"With that cowboy you've been hanging out with?"

"Maybe." Abigail didn't dare answer affirmatively for fear that Grant would also become a target. But her answer was yes. She wanted a life away from her family. A life filled with love and security.

The man pulled off his mask and revealed a

tanned face with dark hair, dark eyes, and a scar across the cheek.

As the man glanced at his phone again, Abigail saw a slight smile curl the edge of his lips.

He was counting on Grant and the gang tracing him back to this house, wasn't he?

And the only reason he would count on that would be if he had something else planned—something bad.

Another booby trap?

A sick feeling swirled in Abigail's gut.

It was the only thing that made sense.

How in the world was she going to protect Grant and his friends?

She had no idea.

"WE GOT a ping on the location of the phone this guy left with Abigail," Dash said over the phone.

"She has it with her?" Grant asked.

"That's how it appears. It looks like it's coming from a house up . . . up in the area where their resort is planned to be built."

Grant paused near the door to the Ferguson's

place and let that sink in. Why would she have her phone with her? What sense did that make?

It didn't matter. What mattered was that they had a location.

A few houses were out in that area, Grant realized. Mostly old fishing and hunting cabins that had been abandoned for years.

That might make it the perfect location to hide away.

"I'm headed there now." Grant opened the door.

"What about us?" Mr. Ferguson rose from the couch, the wrinkles on his forehead deepening.

Grant glanced back at Abigail's parents, realizing that beneath their pious apathy was a hint of worry. "You stay here with the doors locked and your bodyguards intact. I'll keep in touch."

The last thing Grant needed was for them to get in his way. They'd already caused enough trouble.

Mr. Ferguson nodded. "But what about the money?"

"You still have an hour to send it," Grant said. "Have the funds ready, just in case. Of course, we never recommend actually sending the money. It hardly ever works out. This man has another agenda."

They'd already looked into Joseph's background

and had discovered he'd been a weapons specialist for the Navy. He fit all of the criteria right now to be the bad guy. He'd also been dishonorably discharged from the military for erratic behavior.

They'd thought about calling Lucia to see if she could talk some sense into him. But they'd learned she died a year ago.

Grant had to wonder if that was part of what had spurred this guy on to do what he was doing now. No doubt he was bitter.

Grant climbed into his truck and took off toward the house. It was probably only about fifteen minutes away. Levi and Dash were headed there also.

He needed to reach it quickly.

The sun was just beginning to come up. Normally, Grant thought of the early rays of sunlight as a sign of hope for a new day. He prayed that was what they meant now also.

But he knew that there was a chance that things could turn ugly.

He also knew that despite all his differences with Abigail, he cared about her deeply. There were some things in life that were more important than stances they took on earthly events. Sometimes, when two hearts connected, it was worth the risk to see if things could work.

Grant hoped they all survived long enough to take that risk.

As the house came into view, he stopped a safe distance away. He didn't want to give this guy too much notification that they were here.

Levi and Dash pulled up at the same time he did.

The three of them drew their weapons as they started toward the house.

More backup would be here soon.

But for now, they had to get Abigail out of there before it was too late.

CHAPTER FORTY-FOUR

"YOU DON'T HAVE to hurt people, you know." Abigail stared at Joseph, knowing it was a long shot that she might change his mind. But she needed to try anyway.

"I tried the business tactics that your father seemed to love," Joseph snapped. "I demanded that he give me my way. Money was involved. And nothing happened. So now I have to resort to these measures."

"Why bring yourself down to my dad's level?"

Joseph shrugged. "Why not? It seemed to have worked out well for him—except for the fact he's in deep financial trouble right now."

Abigail sucked in a quick breath. "What do you mean?"

"You don't know, do you?" A smile tugged at his lips.

"Know what?" What did he know about her father that Abigail didn't?

"Your dad is in deep with his gambling debt. He has no money. That's why he's hedging everything on this resort. He needs to build it, open it, and hope it turns a profit if he wants to maintain the lifestyle you guys have now."

"No . . ." Abigail shook her head. She would know that if it was the truth. There would have been hints . . . right?

Wait. She stilled.

Although she didn't know much about her father's financial situation, he *had* hinted that he needed the resort to be built to fulfill some type of monetary obligation. She remembered telling Grant about it.

Could Father have a gambling problem? Even with all the things she'd come to know about him, she didn't want to believe it.

Joseph shrugged. "Fine. Have it your way. You'll see."

"My father doesn't gamble."

"You believe that. But I've been following your dad for the past year, trying to come up with my plan. He does gamble. I also know about your mom. She has MS. Her treatments are going to get expensive, and it certainly would be a shame if your father couldn't afford them."

She sucked in a sharp breath. "How do you know that?"

Joseph smirked. "I was military. I worked in counterintelligence. I not only know how to develop weapons, but I also know all about technology. I know about listening devices and cameras. I've been keeping an eye on your family for a while."

"You're better than this," she told him, desperate to get through to him. "There are other ways to get justice."

"It's not like I can exactly take your father to court for firing my mother."

"No, but you're smart. If my father has been doing illegal things, figure out what they are. Use those against him."

"People like me never win against people like your father. You can't even deny that that's true."

Abigail opened her mouth, wanting to deny that very thing. But she couldn't. She knew what money could buy.

Almost anything . . . except happiness.

Before they could talk any longer, she heard a creak on the front porch.

As a smile spread across Joseph's face, Abigail braced herself for whatever would happen next.

And she prayed fervently that God would protect her protectors.

<hr>

GRANT STEPPED ON THE PORCH, checking the boards beneath him to make sure there weren't any trapdoors.

It felt solid.

As he glanced up, he didn't see any cameras either.

They were going to try a different approach.

Levi had agreed that Grant could be their spokesman. For now.

He knocked on the door, tension threaded through his body. "Joseph, we know you're in there. We need to talk."

He waited, unsure if the man would respond or not. But the next moment, someone spoke.

"I'm not in the mood to talk," a deep voice said. "I don't want you here."

Hope rose in Grant.

They were here.

Now he just needed to rescue the woman he loved.

"Abigail doesn't have anything to do with this, Joseph," Grant said. "Why don't you let her go?"

"Because then I will have no leverage. You know that."

Grant leaned closer to the wooden door with the chipped orange paint. "Right now, no one's been killed. You could still walk away from this with only a few years in jail. But if you harm Abigail . . . you're going to be going away for a long time."

Grant suspected this man had killed Merle as well, but he wouldn't bring that up now. He needed this man to feel more powerful than he actually was.

"I have nothing left to keep me wanting to continue with my life the way it's been," Joseph said. "Jail doesn't scare me."

"Then what about Sarah?"

Joseph didn't respond right away. That's when Grant knew he had him.

"How do you know about Sarah?" Joseph finally asked, something close to anger simmering in his voice.

"She needs a father, Joseph. She needs you."

"Her mother thinks I've lost my mind." Joseph's

words came out more quickly. "She won't let me see her."

"Then you can fight it," Grant said.

"Not if I'm in jail. And let's face it, either way, I'm going to end up in jail."

"If you stop now, you could be out in a few years. You'll have a chance to make things right. Don't mess this up, Joseph." Grant prayed that he would get through to this man.

"You weren't supposed to know about Sarah." Joseph's voice wavered with building emotion.

"What kind of cop would I be if I didn't do my research?" Grant gripped his gun, ready to act if necessary. He hoped they could talk this through, but he knew that wasn't likely. "Let Abigail go. Then you and I can have a talk."

"What if I don't want to?"

"Don't make the situation escalate," Grant said.

"It looks like it is too late for that."

What did that mean? Was Abigail okay? Maybe he should ask for proof of life.

Before Grant could fully think this plan through, smoke began to rise around him.

Smoke? Or was that gas?

Something must have been triggered from

beneath the deck. Now the fumes crept up from the boards.

This was why Abigail had that phone. This guy had wanted them to find him. He had more traps set up, didn't he?

Grant coughed, his eyes stinging as the gas irritated him.

Against his better wishes, he backed away from the front door.

He'd be no good to Abigail if he couldn't see or breathe.

But he was a long way from giving up.

He coughed again and retreated—but only temporarily. This battle was far from being over.

CHAPTER FORTY-FIVE

"WHAT DID YOU DO TO HIM?" Abigail asked.

Joseph's eyes sparked with life and his voice nearly sounded jolly as he said, "Just a little gas. The fun is just getting started."

She had to think of a way to convince him this was wrong. "Joseph, what would your mom think about all of this?"

The smile disappeared from his face as he loomed over her. "Don't bring her into this."

"You're the one who brought her into this. You said she's the reason you're doing this now—because of the way my father treated her. But I remember what a great woman your mom was. She would never approve of this."

"Shut up!" His nostrils flared.

"You know it's true," Abigail continued. "She's probably looking down from heaven right now shaking her head."

"I said shut up!" Joseph stormed closer and slapped the gun across her face.

Abigail fought a cry as pain spread through her cheekbone. Blood flooded her mouth.

She should have expected that.

But Abigail hadn't anticipated how much it would take her breath away.

"I don't want you to mention my mom again." Joseph glared at her from above.

Abigail wanted to keep talking about Lucia. But she knew it wouldn't be in her best interest to do so. This guy was on the verge of losing it.

Instead, she sat quietly for a moment. What would Joseph do next?

She really didn't want to find out. But she had no choice.

How else could this guy have booby trapped the place?

She glanced around, trying to spot any signs of what he might have planned.

Numerous things sat on the kitchen table, mostly things she couldn't identify—wires and radios and tools.

When she put those together, what did she have?

Certainly, Joseph wasn't creating a bomb. Why would he blow this whole place up with him still inside?

Unless this wasn't about the money.

Joseph already said he didn't care if he spent the rest of his days in jail. Did that mean he also didn't care if he died?

But then why would he want her father's money? There must be a small part of him that wanted to stay alive, to prove himself.

Her thoughts swirled.

Abigail licked her lips, deciding to try a different approach. "How old is Sarah?"

Joseph glanced back at her, anger glowing in his eyes. "I don't want to talk about her."

"Five hundred thousand dollars would let you do a lot of things. You could take her on trips. Buy a house. Make a nice life for yourself."

"It doesn't look like that's going to be happening." His voice cracked.

She'd found his weak spot, she realized. Some in the crisis management field would tell her to exploit it, to deflect attention from herself. It wasn't her usual tactic, but her life was on the line.

"What if you could get away from here?" Abigail

asked. "With the money? If you let me negotiate and be on your side, maybe I can help."

He froze and stared at her. "You would do that?"

"It's kind of what I'm trained in. I know how to handle crisis situations. I could help you."

"But why would you?"

Abigail shrugged. "Because I don't want to see my father get away with that either. I want to do something for Lucia. What happened to her was wrong. But there's got to be a better way to do this."

"Then what do you propose?" Joseph narrowed his eyes as he waited for her to continue.

Abigail's thoughts raced. She needed to come up with that crisis management plan.

Now.

* * *

"JOSEPH, you don't want to do this!" Grant called, staying a safe distance from the front door.

Who knew what else this guy had planned?

Silence answered Grant.

What was going on in that old cottage? Grant felt certain that both Joseph and Abigail were inside.

He glanced at Levi, who gave him a nod, indicating he should continue.

"Can we talk, Joseph?" Grant asked. "We don't want this to escalate any more than you do."

No one answered again.

More apprehension built in Grant, and his heart pounded more quickly against his chest.

His phone buzzed. As he glanced at his screen, he saw it was Thomas Ferguson.

"Should I send the money?" Mr. Ferguson asked.

Grant's jaw tightened. He didn't know what to tell the man. Grant would do anything to keep Abigail safe. But he couldn't read Joseph yet. He didn't know enough about him.

Would getting the money end with Joseph killing Abigail?

Grant didn't know, but he didn't see a happy ending to this.

Just then, bangs filled the air.

Something hit the sand around him.

Bullets.

Someone was shooting.

Grant ducked behind his truck.

Where were they even coming from?

He wasn't sure. But this guy had anticipated them coming.

And now he was enacting the last part of his plan.

CHAPTER FORTY-SIX

ADRENALINE SURGED through Abigail as she heard the gunfire outside. What was that?

"Do you have more guys working for you?" She tried to wrap her mind around the situation, to get some kind of handle on what was going on.

Joseph grinned as he remained in front of her, his phone in his hand. "No, those are some automatic weapons I set up. I control them with just a push of a button here on my phone. Pretty amazing, huh?"

"That's sick." How could this man be so cruel? How had bitterness consumed him so much?

"Sick but effective. Usually, people who can't go out to hunt set them up. I found other uses for the technology, however."

Abigail's mind raced. What if Grant or one of his friends had been hit? She could hardly bear the thought.

Her gaze nearly burned into Joseph as she glanced back at him. "I thought we were going to talk about a crisis management plan?"

"We were, but you didn't say anything."

This man needed help. That was clear.

"We can't stay here forever." Abigail tugged against her binds, but it was no use. The ropes were too tight. "They're going to have this place surrounded. That's going to result in an hours-long standoff. No one wants that, right?"

"Then what do you propose, Ms. Ferguson?" He took his knife and began sharpening it with another tool he pulled from his pocket.

"I think you should get out of here. Use me as a shield. They won't be able to shoot you. You go to your vehicle—I'm assuming you have one and that's how you got me here—and we leave the island." She stared at the blade, knowing good and well how deadly it could be.

"Do I need to remind you that you can't drive off this island right now?" He held his knife up and examined it more closely.

Abigail tried to stay focused, to keep her heart

rate down. She looked away from the knife. "They have a temporary bridge up for construction workers. If you go fast enough, nobody will be able to stop you."

"I like the way you think. But what then?" He began working on that blade again, almost as if he knew it would unnerve her.

"Have my dad send you the money. You let me go. And you start a life on your own. Nobody will have to find you."

"Do you really think that that would work?" Doubt tinged his voice.

"You just need to find you a new identity. You can pay cash for a house. This could work. But nobody else needs to get hurt." This was what she did. She managed crises. She had to think of this situation in that way also.

Joseph shrugged, unaffected by the danger crackling around them. "I'm thinking about it."

"Do you have more traps set for the guys outside?" She swallowed hard as she waited for his answer.

"I never give away my secrets."

Abigail didn't like that response. "These guys didn't do anything to you. Why try to hurt them?"

Joseph's gaze flickered up to meet hers. He put

his knife back in its sheath and frowned. "My mom always said you had a good heart. She said that you were different from the rest of your family."

"That's because I am. I think you know that. I'm not like my father."

He stared at her another moment, thoughts brewing in his gaze. "I'm going to think about your plan. But first I have one more trick up my sleeve. It would be a shame if all of this hard work was for nothing."

"You don't have to do this, Joseph."

He smiled again. "But I do. I am sorry, Abigail."

***

GRANT NEEDED to think of a different plan. They couldn't go to the front door. Even though the gas would dissipate into the air, they couldn't take that chance.

If they went beneath the house, they'd be out of the range of fire.

But was there risk in that also?

If Grant had to guess, the answer was yes.

Just what did Joseph have planned for them?

Grant didn't know, and he didn't want to find out.

What he wanted was to get Abigail out of there.

He backed up to the truck where Levi and Dash stood poised to fight. "What do you think?"

Levi frowned. "We can wait for backup to get here, but I'm afraid it's going to be too late."

"If we go back to the front door, then we're going to be in the range of fire again. Plus, he probably has some kind of other surprise for us beneath the house."

"You're probably right," Levi said.

Grant squinted as he stared at the house. "Is that a ... trip wire across the bottom of the house?"

Levi peered beneath the structure and frowned. "It certainly looks like it."

"You think this guy has a bomb set up down there?" Dash asked. "He's the definition of above and beyond."

"It's a good guess that he has some type of explosive device," Levi said. "Maybe not enough to take the house out, but enough to damage the person who trips it."

Grant bit down. This guy really had thought of everything, hadn't he? Part of his enjoyment was taking people by surprise.

"I think we should trigger it," Grant finally said,

still staring at the tripwire. "Make this guy think that something happened and that one of us could be hurt."

"How do you propose we do that?" Dash asked.

Grant looked around, his eyes stopping on the spare tire in the back of his truck. "Why don't we roll that into the house and see what happens?"

"What if we're wrong and the explosive is bigger than we think?" Dash asked.

"I don't think it will be." Levi shook his head, his jaw still clenched tight. "This guy wants that money. He wants to get away."

"I think it's worth a shot." Grant looked at Dash. "Do you want to give me a hand?"

"Of course."

The two of them lifted the tire from the truck. Then they pushed it across the ground. When they got close enough to the house, they gave it a good roll and watched as it shot forward. Moving quickly, they ducked back behind their vehicles.

Grant watched as the tire got closer and closer to the trip line. He held his breath as it finally hit the wire.

Just as they expected, a small explosion filled the air.

Thank goodness, none of them had been under there when it happened. Their bodies would definitely suffer from burns.

Now that this booby trap was out of the way, they needed to think of their next step.

CHAPTER FORTY-SEVEN

"WHAT WAS THAT SOUND?" Abigail felt adrenaline burst inside her. This guy . . . he just never seemed to stop. He'd practically set up a minefield outside, hadn't he?

"Tripwire." He grinned. "I put it beneath the house. I figured they'd go under there."

Her head began to spin at the thought. What if someone had gotten hurt while trying to rescue her? That wasn't what she wanted.

"That's cruel, Joseph," she finally muttered. "You're not a cruel person."

"That's what my mom used to always say too. It looks like she was wrong." He rubbed his jaw, as if the thought made him unhappy.

She needed to strike now, while he was feeling

sentimental—or maybe regretting his actions. "Have you thought about my offer?"

"You think I can leave here with you? And, when I do, you're going to help me get that money and start a new life for myself?"

"That's right."

He stared at her, his eyes nearly devoid of any compassion or empathy. "What's in it for you?"

"I just don't want to see you hurt anybody else."

"And that's it?"

"Isn't that enough?"

He stared at her a moment, and Abigail couldn't read his expression. She had no idea what the man was thinking right now.

Finally, he nodded. "You're right. The longer we wait here, the more time these guys have to plan whatever it is they are going to do. Maybe our best bet is just to get out of here. Besides, they've already been through all my hidden deterrents. I'm tired of waiting."

Abigail nodded. She hoped she was making the right choice. But what was the right choice in the situation? The only thing she knew was that she needed to keep the people she loved safe.

"Fine, I'll go." He reached for her and jerked her to her feet.

She held her breath as he reached for his knife. She squeezed her eyes shut as he lunged it toward her.

But instead of feeling pain, her wrists were set free.

He'd cut the rope.

The next instance, the knife sliced through the binds at her ankles also.

She was free! For a moment, at least.

Then he jammed his gun into her side. "Don't make any sudden moves."

"I won't." But at least she had a fighting chance now.

He released her just long enough to fish something out of his pocket. A moment later, he pressed some keys into her hand. "You're going to drive so I can keep the gun on you. Plus, you know where this bridge is, right?"

She nodded. "I do."

"Part of me is sorry that I pulled you into this."

There was so much Abigail wanted to say, but she knew that none of it would change his mind. So instead, she nodded. "Are you ready to go?"

"Yes, I am."

With one last glance around the room, Joseph opened the door.

Abigail braced herself for whatever would happen next.

GRANT SAW the door open and gripped his gun.

His heart skipped a beat when he saw Abigail appear.

Joseph was behind her.

With a gun at her side.

Grant's jaw clenched. Just what was this guy planning now?

"Don't make a move!" Joseph called, his teeth looking clenched and his muscles tight and ready to spring. "If you do, I'll shoot her. I mean it."

Abigail looked fine, all things considered, and seemed to be moving okay.

But, still, there was nothing about the situation that Grant liked.

"What do you want?" Grant called.

"Abigail and I are going to go to my truck. We're going to drive away from here. And you're not going to try to stop us. If you do, there will be consequences you won't like. Do you understand?"

Abigail was going to leave this island with the man? Concern ricocheted through Grant. That would only end in disaster. As soon as Joseph got whatever it was that he wanted from her, she'd be dead. He had no doubt about that.

But how could Grant stop them from leaving without getting anyone hurt?

This was what they had trained for. But everything felt different when someone you cared about was in the line of fire.

"Are you sure we can't talk?" Levi called.

"I've done enough talking," Joseph said. "The best thing that can happen is that Thomas Ferguson sends me the money I requested."

Joseph kept moving forward, down the stairs.

Abigail looked tense as she took each step carefully, as if afraid one slipup might result in him pulling the trigger.

Grant wanted to reach out to her. He wanted to pull her into the safety of his arms. Wanted to get her away from that madman.

But that wasn't possible right now.

The gun in Joseph's hand changed everything.

"You guys need to back up," Joseph said. "No sudden moves."

They did as he asked and stepped behind their vehicles.

Grant's gaze went to the man's truck. It was

parked right in front of the steps. As soon as Joseph and Abigail reached the bottom, they'd be able to climb in.

Was there something he could do to stop them?

That was what he needed to figure out.

"Grant," Abigail said, her voice shaky.

His heart pounded in his ears. "Yes?"

"Thank you for everything."

He knew what that meant. Abigail didn't think she would ever see him again.

Grant couldn't let that happen.

"Don't say goodbye to me, Abigail," he told her.

Her gaze met his, and, without saying a word, millions of conversations were spoken.

Grant knew without a doubt that Abigail cared about him. He cared about her also. They could have a really beautiful future together. Sure, they had issues to work through. But didn't every couple?

They'd come this far, and Grant wasn't going to lose her now.

"Enough of this Hallmark moment," Joseph muttered. "I'm watching all of you. No sudden moves."

Just as he said those words, movement in the distance caught Grant's eye. He glanced beside him, wondering what new surprise was headed their way now.

A figure lumbered down the road.

Grant braced himself.

Who was here?

And what would that mean for Abigail?

CHAPTER FORTY-EIGHT

ABIGAIL'S EYES widened when she saw Johnny walking toward them. He had Air Pods in his ears and sunglasses on as he moseyed down the road.

Her brother was clueless. He had no idea what was going on, did he?

Now he could ruin all of this.

Joseph dug the gun harder into her ribs.

She was keenly aware of the weapon, keenly aware that one slip of his finger could end everything for her.

Everything seemed to happen in slow motion.

Johnny looked up.

Saw what was happening.

Froze.

Joseph pulled his gun away from her and aimed it at her brother.

She held her breath, unsure what exactly was happening.

The next instant, gunfire exploded around her.

She froze, waiting to feel the pain. Waiting for everything to go still around her. Waiting to breathe her last breath.

Instead, Joseph sank to the ground beside her.

He gasped as he grabbed his chest and looked up at her, almost as if trying to communicate one final message.

She clutched her throat, horrified as she watched life slip away from her abductor.

As his fingers moved, her eyes went to the gun beside him.

Even in his dying moment, he still wanted revenge, didn't he?

Moving quickly, she kicked it out of the way.

As she did, her knees seemed to turn to gelatin.

But before she hit the ground, strong arms caught her from behind.

Grant.

She was safe.

She was finally safe.

AS GRANT WATCHED EVERYTHING HAPPENING, he knew he had no choice but to act.

Otherwise, Joseph was going to shoot Johnny.

That was why, when he'd seen the opportunity to stop Joseph, he had to take it.

He'd pulled the trigger, and his bullet hit Joseph in the chest.

The man sank to the ground, still alive but gasping for breath.

Beside him, Levi called for more backup.

Grant rushed across the sandy ground. He reached Abigail just as she kicked the gun away.

He sensed her strength was waning, and his arms encircled her just as her legs went weak.

"Grant?" She looked up at him, her limbs feeling limp.

"It's okay now," he murmured. "I've got you."

Abigail let out a little muffled cry and buried her head into his chest.

As Grant held her, he vowed to never let her go.

He glanced down at Joseph. The man was still alive.

Dash and Levi rushed forward to attend to him.

Things could have turned out much differently.

Grant knew that. He was grateful to have another chance.

"I knew you'd come for me," Abigail said.

Grant held her closer. "Always. I'll always come for you, Abigail."

CHAPTER FORTY-NINE

AS THE SUN set on the west side of the island, Abigail stood in front of Grant. His arms wrapped around her waist as they stared out over the wild horses roaming the beach in the distance.

Grant raised an arm and pointed at one of the horses. "Remember the mare I told you about who escaped and was eventually found integrated with the wild horses? Wanderlust?"

"I do."

"That's her."

Abigail's gaze fell on the chestnut mare as she ran alongside two other horses.

"She blends in well," Abigail said. "You can hardly tell she hasn't always been a part of the harem."

"It's true, isn't it?"

A lot had happened over the past few months.

Thomas Ferguson had been arrested. Investigators had filed several charges against him, including blackmail. He had, indeed, been trying to pay off county council members in order to get the permits that he needed. It also turned out that he had a large gambling debt and had funneled money from some of his clients' accounts in order to pay off his own debt.

It was one of the primary reasons that her father had wanted to start this resort. If he could find the right investors, then he could build it and make back the funding he needed to pay off the debt collectors who were hounding him.

Abigail's mother had moved back to New York to live with her sister there. She said that this place caused her too many bad memories.

Abigail thought it was a good move for her mom to be with her sister at a time like this. Both Abigail and her mom were still trying to work through things after Abigail's abduction.

Johnny had decided to visit his friends around the country. Abigail suspected that soon his trust fund would run out and her brother would have to get himself a real job. He was apparently going to enjoy every moment until that happened.

Abigail, on the other hand, had decided to remain permanently in Cape Corral. She was starting her own public relations firm, but she would work virtually from the little cottage she was renting here. She was still trying to get on her own feet, but so far so good.

Grant leaned closer until his head was right next to hers. "I love you, Abigail Ferguson."

She turned her gaze away from the horses until she faced him. "I love you too, Grant Matthews."

"Have I ever told you how beautiful you are?"

"Pretty as a peach? Or finer than a frog hair split four ways?"

"Both of those. A million times over."

A smile spread across Abigail's face. She was so glad God had brought Grant into her life.

Though there had been a few rocky moments as she'd integrated into the community, overall, things had gone incredibly well. Grant's friends had pulled her into their circle and accepted her as one of their own.

Abigail had even been going to church regularly and eating at The Screen Porch Café. Grant was right. Mrs. Minnie's crab cakes were to die for.

Grant took a step back and glanced at the time before taking one of her hands. "We probably need to get seated for Dash and Lizzie's wedding."

"Yes, we do."

As a wedding gift, Dash had bought Lizzie some of the property Thomas Ferguson had once owned. Dash was making it into a preserve for the horses. If everything went according to plan, this space would become a sanctuary and no one would ever be allowed to build here on the northern banks.

Abigail was so glad. Though she had been on the fence at first, now she could see why these horses needed space to run free.

"I can't wait to go see the two of them say I do," Abigail said.

"And Preston is going to be the ring bearer," Grant said. "So you know that's going to be a hoot."

Preston was Lizzie's son, and the boy was a true character.

They turned away from the horse sanctuary and headed toward the beach where everybody else was waiting.

She smiled when she saw all the cowboy hats atop heads in the little white wooden chairs on the shoreline. She would have never thought she would go to an island in North Carolina and find cowboys.

But she had.

But, mostly, she was so glad that she had found Grant and had been given a new opportunity for a fresh start.

Abigail felt a little like that driftwood that formed an arch over the makeshift altar on the beach. Dash and Lizzie would get married beneath it with Pastor Daniels presiding over the ceremony.

A storm had pulled those broken branches into the sea where the water had worn down all the rough edges. The end result was smooth wood that was treasured by collectors and artists.

Abigail had been through storms, but they were only going to make her more beautiful. That was her resolve.

She squeezed Grant's hand as she joined the rest of the gang for Dash and Lizzie's happy-ever-after.

~~~

~~~

Thank you so much for reading *Driftwood Danger*. If you enjoyed this book, I would love for you to leave a review! Reviews are a huge help for authors.

To keep up with all the latest news, sign up for my newsletter at: www.christybarritt.com.

COMPLETE BOOK LIST

Squeaky Clean Mysteries:

#1 Hazardous Duty

#2 Suspicious Minds

#2.5 It Came Upon a Midnight Crime (novella)

#3 Organized Grime

#4 Dirty Deeds

#5 The Scum of All Fears

#6 To Love, Honor and Perish

#7 Mucky Streak

#8 Foul Play

#9 Broom & Gloom

#10 Dust and Obey

#11 Thrill Squeaker

#11.5 Swept Away (novella)

#12 Cunning Attractions

#13 Cold Case: Clean Getaway

#14 Cold Case: Clean Sweep

#15 Cold Case: Clean Break

#16 Cleans to an End (coming soon)

While You Were Sweeping, A Riley Thomas Spinoff

The Sierra Files:

#1 Pounced

#2 Hunted

#3 Pranced

#4 Rattled

The Gabby St. Claire Diaries (a Tween Mystery series):

The Curtain Call Caper

The Disappearing Dog Dilemma

The Bungled Bike Burglaries

The Worst Detective Ever

#1 Ready to Fumble

#2 Reign of Error

#3 Safety in Blunders

#4 Join the Flub

#5 Blooper Freak

#6 Flaw Abiding Citizen

#7 Gaffe Out Loud

#8 Joke and Dagger

#9 Wreck the Halls

#10 Glitch and Famous (coming soon)

Raven Remington

Relentless 1

Relentless 2 (coming soon)

Holly Anna Paladin Mysteries:

#1 Random Acts of Murder

#2 Random Acts of Deceit

#2.5 Random Acts of Scrooge

#3 Random Acts of Malice

#4 Random Acts of Greed

#5 Random Acts of Fraud

#6 Random Acts of Outrage

#7 Random Acts of Iniquity

Lantern Beach Mysteries

#1 Hidden Currents

#2 Flood Watch

#3 Storm Surge

#4 Dangerous Waters

#5 Perilous Riptide

#6 Deadly Undertow

Lantern Beach Romantic Suspense

Tides of Deception

Shadow of Intrigue

Storm of Doubt

Winds of Danger

Rains of Remorse

Torrents of Fear

Lantern Beach P.D.

On the Lookout

Attempt to Locate

First Degree Murder

Dead on Arrival

Plan of Action

Lantern Beach Escape

Afterglow (a novelette)

Lantern Beach Blackout

Dark Water

Safe Harbor

Ripple Effect

Rising Tide

Crime á la Mode

Deadman's Float

Milkshake Up

Bomb Pop Threat

Banana Split Personalities

The Sidekick's Survival Guide

The Art of Eavesdropping

The Perks of Meddling

The Exercise of Interfering

The Practice of Prying

The Skill of Snooping

The Craft of Being Covert

Saltwater Cowboys

Saltwater Cowboy

Breakwater Protector

Cape Corral Keeper

Seagrass Secrets

Driftwood Danger

Carolina Moon Series

Home Before Dark

Gone By Dark

Wait Until Dark

Light the Dark

Taken By Dark

Suburban Sleuth Mysteries:

Death of the Couch Potato's Wife

Fog Lake Suspense:

Edge of Peril

Margin of Error

Brink of Danger

Line of Duty

Cape Thomas Series:

Dubiosity

Disillusioned

Distorted

Standalone Romantic Mystery:

The Good Girl

Suspense:

Imperfect

The Wrecking

Sweet Christmas Novella:

Home to Chestnut Grove

Standalone Romantic-Suspense:

Keeping Guard

The Last Target

Race Against Time

Ricochet

Key Witness

Lifeline

High-Stakes Holiday Reunion

Desperate Measures

Hidden Agenda

Mountain Hideaway

Dark Harbor

Shadow of Suspicion

The Baby Assignment

The Cradle Conspiracy

Trained to Defend

Mountain Survival (coming soon)

Nonfiction:

Characters in the Kitchen

Changed: True Stories of Finding God through Christian Music (out of print)

The Novel in Me: The Beginner's Guide to Writing and Publishing a Novel (out of print)

USA Today has called Christy Barritt's books "scary, funny, passionate, and quirky."

Christy writes both mystery and romantic suspense novels that are clean with underlying messages of faith. Her books have won the Daphne du Maurier Award for Excellence in Suspense and Mystery, have been twice nominated for the Romantic Times Reviewers' Choice Award, and have finaled for both a Carol Award and Foreword Magazine's Book of the Year.

She is married to her Prince Charming, a man who thinks she's hilarious—but only when she's not trying to be. Christy is a self-proclaimed klutz, an avid music lover who's known for spontaneously bursting into song, and a road trip aficionado.

When she's not working or spending time with her family, she enjoys singing, playing the guitar, and exploring small, unsuspecting towns where people have no idea how accident-prone she is.

Find Christy online at:

www.christybarritt.com

www.facebook.com/christybarritt

www.twitter.com/cbarritt

Sign up for Christy's newsletter to get information on all of her latest releases here: **www. christybarritt.com/newsletter-sign-up/**

If you enjoyed this book, please consider leaving a review.